THE CHARM OF YOU

A LADIES WHO WRITE Novel
by Jennifer Probst

xoxo *Jennifer Probst*

PRAISE FOR JENNIFER PROBST

"For a sexy, fun-filled, warmhearted read, look no further than Jennifer Probst!"

—Jill Shalvis, *New York Times* bestselling author

"Jennifer Probst is an absolute auto-buy author for me."

—J. Kenner, *New York Times* bestselling author

"Jennifer Probst knows how to bring the swoons and the sexy."

—Amy E. Reichert, author of *The Coincidence of Coconut Cake*

"Jennifer Probst never fails to deliver romance that sizzles and has a way of tugging those emotional heartstrings."

Published by Triple J. Publishing, Inc.
Cover design by Sara Eilrew
Cover photography by Sara Eilrew
Printed in the United States of America

For the founding members of the Ladies Who Write—Marina Adair, Sawyer Bennett, Emma Chase, Melissa Foster, Kristen Proby, and Jill Shalvis
Thank you for all your love and support. I've adored every moment of this journey together!

And for all the readers out there who struggle to believe in themselves; who struggle to reach their dreams; who burn quietly for MORE— never give up. The world needs you.
The world is waiting for you.

"But mostly, I hate the way I don't even hate you. Not even close, not even a little bit, not even at all." – 10 Things I Hate About You

"I'm not running away."
"Bullshit."
–How To Lose A Guy In Ten Days

THE CHARM OF YOU

Jennifer Probst

CHAPTER 1

"I HAVE SOMETHING TO TELL YOU."

Presley Cabot stared at her friend from across her sleek, espresso desk and wondered why she suddenly felt poised at the edge of a roller coaster hill, hovering at the tip, ready to fall to crashing depths at the slightest tap. Her tummy clenched. "Just tell me you're not sick and no one died."

Trinity dropped in the chair opposite her desk and groaned. Her long-limbed body looked squashed in the fashionably designed but small cranberry chair. She didn't seem to care, choosing to hook one leather clad leg over the arm, her feet baring bad-ass black strappy wedges jiggling nonstop. Her snug hot pink t-shirt screamed *Bend the Knee* from Game of Thrones. "No, nothing like that. Why are you always so dramatic?"

"Are you kidding? You live drama. Why are you wearing leather when it's going to be in the seventies today?"

Her friend gave an elegant shrug. "I'm feeling needy and

pathetic so I needed to change my energy. And I don't live drama. I just engage whole-heartedly in this thing called life."

Presley tried not to grin. The moment Trinity walked into a room, her entire aura screamed high maintenance. If she wore a warning label, it would read, *'Proceed with caution.'* But she had the biggest, mushiest heart hidden beneath all that gorgeousness, which made Presley protective over who her friend chose to love. "I engage. But I like to get straight to the truth without delay," she explained. "Rip off the band aid. None of that pansy ass pampering or pulling it off inch by inch, hoping it will dull the pain. No bullshit with me."

"Nolan Banks is back in town."

And just like that, Presley wished she'd prepared herself a bit before the explosion.

His name seared into her mind like a tattoo, launching a pit of memories she'd buried deep and hoped to never unearth. Her body short-circuited like a cut wire suddenly unable to function. The image of those laughing blue eyes nailing her with his stare. The crooked, charming smile. The hard, sleek muscles and ripped abs. The smell of his skin—freshly washed cotton and the delicious mix of sunshine and ocean from his cologne. The years fell away and she was once again that awkward, overweight college student no one ever acknowledged.

Until Nolan talked to her that one night.

So, she'd slept with him.

And he'd destroyed her.

"Uh, oh. You have that look in your eye," Trinity said, a worry glint in her chocolate brown eyes. Her foot jiggled faster. "Breathe, girlfriend. Just take some deep breaths."

"Why didn't I know? Why wasn't I told?" She rattled off

questions like bullets, her mind madly buzzing. "Why did Aubrey keep this a secret and why did Libby let her?" Her two best friends knew all about her past with Nolan. Presley assumed they'd be the ones to break the news.

Trinity held up one elegant hand, her Pandora bracelets clicking together. "You've been in Europe, remember? I was not about to mess with your mojo by telling you this from overseas. Aubrey's been visiting Charlotte for a well needed break, and Libby got involved with another fundraiser in Chicago. I figured I'd break the news the moment you got back. I'm kind of surprised you didn't hear the gossip, though. It's been buzzing in Port Hudson for weeks about the old dive bar being taken over by a new owner. How was Italy, by the way? Did you bring me new shoes?"

"Yes, of course. Now, give me a moment as my head is spinning. I need to focus."

Gripping the edge of the desk and forcing oxygen into her lungs, Presley tried to steady herself. *Ridiculous*. It'd been almost a decade since they've seen each other. She was over the humiliation. She'd moved on and kicked ass with her life. Lost a hundred pounds. Became one of the richest CEO's in America with the world at her feet. She dated anyone who caught her fancy because, finally, she got to choose.

Yet the sound of his name rattling in her brain was enough to make all her damn girly parts tingle.

Bastard.

Trinity snapped her fingers, her scarlet-tipped nails flashing in the air. "There you are! Anger is good. Anger is real. Let the hate flow so you can clear out those junk emotions and begin moving forward."

Presley groaned, launching up from her chair to pace her

modern, lush office like a caged animal. "Damnit, I should have been back last week but I had to check on one of my writers who's late on her deadline. She's hiding in the deep South because she's afraid of the blowback from her tell-all."

Trinity licked her lush lips. "Did she sleep with him? Tell me!"

"Buy the book."

"Bitch."

"Tell me everything," Presley demanded. "Every last detail. Why is he back? When is he leaving? Is he married? Is he bald and fat? Why aren't you talking?"

Her friend let out a long-suffering sigh, crossed her arms over her ample breasts, and began rattling off the information. "He showed up a month ago, took down the For Sale sign for the Bucket Hole bar, and began renovation. He's making it into a pub and small microbrewery. He's staying in town permanently and rented one of those apartments close to town. He's single and unfortunately, he's still hot."

Presley froze mid-stride. "He's staying permanently?" she asked softly. Her heart squeezed, paused, then raced into overdrive. "He's going to be sharing my town?"

"Technically, Port Hudson isn't your town, though you could probably buy it and kick him out. Want me to begin checking on the details of that move?"

"No, then he'd know I actually thought about him over all these years and I'd die of humiliation. His ego is probably already inflated enough without any help from me."

"True. Want me to see if he needs money to borrow? I can call Jack. He'll offer him an ungodly amount of money at high interest, call on the debt early, and threaten to break his knee caps."

4

Presley rubbed her temples, trying hard to think if that was an option. "No, I can't get behind causing physical harm even for him. Jack still does that?"

"Hmmm, he comes in handy."

"Good to know. Wait a minute . . . his brother Carter owns the pub, Quarters. Why is Nolan opening up another bar in the same town?"

Trinity grinned. "'Cause they're both crazy competitive with each other. Word on the street is Nolan ditched his financial career on Wall Street to open up a brewery with an exclusive bar menu. Think beer and food pairing instead of wine. He's calling it The Bank. A few people have said he's offering some amazing brews. God knows we needed some decent beer and cocktails in this area. The damn college students can only afford the brands that taste like piss because they're broke."

Presley grinned. "Like we did?"

"We had better taste when we attended Boyer University."

"Slow Gin Fizzes is better taste?"

Trinity shuddered. "Don't remind me. I still can't look at them without getting nauseous after drinking ten that night."

Presley tapped her finger against her lips and spun around on her heel. "I know what I have to do."

Fortunately, her friend knew enough to follow her bouncing thoughts. "Try to buy the bar out from under him and fire his ass?"

"No, but that idea is tempting. I need to walk in there like I barely remember him. Like he's a bug underneath my Pradas. Like our night together and his cruel behavior afterwards meant nothing. It's the only way to exorcise his ghost."

Trinity's eyes softened as she met her gaze. "You never got

over him, did you?" she asked softly. "Even after what he did? Even after everything you proved and accomplished?"

Emotion tightened her throat. How badly she wanted to lie and say yes, she had. That she never remembered how fiercely she adored Nolan Banks for two years, or how important their night together was. She pretended the ease with which he'd squashed the broken remnants of her heart was forgotten. After all, she'd grown into the woman she was today after a hell of a lot of hard work, sweat, and tears. Her tight circle of friends and sorority sisters of Ladies Who Write not only encouraged her to be the woman she dreamed of, but accepted her exactly the way she was.

When she first entered Boyer University, it'd been difficult to find friends and fit into a group. She'd met Libby and Aubrey in Creative Writing 101, and had immediately bonded with their shared love of writing. The three of them became like sisters, but none of the groups or sororities on campus seemed to fit them. One drunken night after too many shots, they all decided to found their own sorority called The Ladies Who Write. It had been an instant success and over the years, the sisterhood had grown in numbers, with graduates working all over the world, yet still feeling bonded to the group as a whole.

Presley smiled at the memory. She'd blossomed once she found a tight circle of friends who accepted and embraced who she was. If only it hadn't been for that damn party.

But deep inside, the wound had not scarred over cleanly. When she slept, he still showed up in her dreams, tempting her to step into his arms and trust him one last time. In the dreams, she did. In the dreams, she obviously lost all common sense.

Because the asshole betrayed her again.

Maybe this was her opportunity to close an important

chapter in her life. She'd never forgive him, but she could move on. Confirm those feelings were leftover emotions from a lovesick, scared, shy college student who wasn't ready yet to leap into her future and fly.

Maybe it was time to prove the Nolan Banks she thought she loved had never been real.

"Pres?"

She shook off her thoughts and re-focused on her friend. "Most of the time I do," she said truthfully. "But sometimes, the past tries to rear up and trick me into believing I got lucky. That I'm not worth it. That everyone will know I'm not the glamourous, fabulous CEO of LWW Enterprises. I'm just that fat, shy, and awkward girl begging people to love her."

Silence fell. Trinity regarded her for a while, not afraid of letting the raw emotions in the room run its course. Finally, she nodded. "I get it. But you can't go see him in that."

Presley looked down at her outfit—a smart, Vera Wang business suit in smoke gray. "What's wrong? I thought you approved of this outfit."

"I do, but not for man hunting. That suit's all business when you need something that screams *pleasure*. Or more like, making him regret the day he crapped all over you. Wait until tomorrow—I'll send over the perfect outfit. I'll get his schedule so you'll know the right time to coincidentally 'pop in' and check the place out."

A laugh bubbled from her lips. "You don't think I can pick out my own clothes by now?"

Trinity grinned. "I'm still Queen of Fashion, baby. Never gonna give up that title."

Presley had met her friend in the LWW sorority, but it hadn't been until senior year that Trinity approached her with a

7

plan to revamp her look. Graduating with a dual degree in fashion design and psychology, she planned to merge them both into a career that everyone told her was impossible.

Fashion therapist.

Presley had been one of her first clients. After losing a good twenty-five pounds, she'd still been trapped in her old body and mind, unable to move forward in her clothes choices. Trinity had dug deep to find out the type of person Presley had wanted to reflect, then strove to build that woman around her new wardrobe.

It worked. By the time she'd shed the next seventy-five pounds, they'd formed a tight bond. Presley recruited her to write a weekly column on fashion therapy for the LWW magazine and watched as her friend became famous and even been interviewed on *Good Morning America* for her unique career. If Trinity knew the perfect outfit, then it'd be worth waiting for.

"Okay, you win. I hope I'm dazzled."

Her friend flashed her a bright white smile filled with smugness. Her gorgeous hair was done up in elaborate braids that hung down her back and showed off the glow of her black skin. "You will be. Now, are you going to be alright? I'm on deadline for a piece and have a client within the hour."

"I'm fine. Thanks for telling me before someone else caught me by surprise. At least, I can be prepared."

"To meet the man you loved, lost your virginity to, and got humiliated by? Don't think you'll ever be prepared for that, honey." She slid out of the chair and winked. "But at least you can put the hurt on him and maybe a bit of regret in him. Check in with you later."

Blowing her signature kiss, she prowled out of the room, leaving the energy behind her stagnant and grieving her presence. That woman was meant for a man bigger than life, someone who could handle a beautiful, bright, and unabashedly bold woman.

Probably the reason Trinity was still single.

There seemed to be none left.

Presley walked to the window and stared out at the Hudson River in the distance. They'd situated the building close enough for a great view, but not dependent on stripping down acres of land. Built completely environmentally friendly, from solar panels to custom glass paned windows to diminish dependency on oil, LWW Enterprises headquarters was kept small enough not to overtake community life, but brought a decent amount of jobs to the area. An hour from New York City, Port Hudson had commuter trains conveniently close by and was built on the high edge of where the mountains met the river. It wasn't as expensive and trendy as Westchester, and to Presley, it made the place perfect to run a conglomerate. Her friends had a clear vision of what they wanted to achieve and they accomplished it in an impressive manner.

Presley sighed and pressed her forehead to the cool pane of glass. So, why did she still feel like something was missing? Or someone? Because she'd just passed her thirtieth birthday? Hell, she honestly believed she was in her prime and only had more to conquer. But crawling into a cold bed night after night was beginning to grate on her nerves. She craved a connection with a man who *got* her. A man who not only rocked her body and heart, but also her mind. She'd always owned a sarcastic streak, and adored a wicked sense of humor. The last few men she'd taken to her bed had been too easy to leave in the morning. They'd simply bored her and some didn't even care about pleasing her. Her soul searched restlessly for the elusive man who seemed to click with all parts of her.

Did he exist?

The moment she'd laid eyes on Nolan Banks in her freshman year, she'd gotten all the feels. From the shaky knees to the squeeze of her heart, she'd been entranced, sensing deep inside her very soul he was meant for her. He'd set her body on fire and then reduced their connection to ashes, her Prince Charming fleeing before even giving his Princess a chance.

She'd been wrong. Maybe she still hadn't recovered. Maybe finally seeing him again after all these years would give her the closure she'd been desperately needing.

Presley sighed, turned from the window, and got back to work.

CHAPTER 2

"He's here."

Presley froze in the doorway, momentarily stopped by the gorgeous guy with the confident smile who caused her heart to pound out of her chest. He was surrounded by his track crew, leaning against the wall, his fingers holding the neck of a beer bottle. He threw his head back and laughed at something one of the guys said. His curly oak-brown hair flopped over his brow, and he unconsciously swept it away, a gesture he'd made about a thousand times per day. Even from this distance, she caught the spark in those navy blue eyes. Her gaze feasted on the perfect angles to his face. Square jaw. Strong nose. The thin, defined upper lip only emphasized the delicious fullness of his lower one. And his body? Rock hard and lean. Long, muscular legs that could eat up a track with heart-stopping swiftness. Abs that a quarter could bounce on. She knew—because his jock friends had dared him to shed his shirt so they could test it out.

The quarter bounced.

She grew achy between her thighs, which smooshed together

uncomfortably in the short, black dress her friends forced her to wear. Trying hard not to make a fool out of herself and drool, she pretended she didn't see him, but she couldn't hide her reaction from her friends who saw right through her.

"Told you he'd be here," Aubrey said smugly. "This is his friend's house and a frat brother. You're going to talk to him tonight, Pres. I know you can do this."

Libby shot her a sympathetic smile. "Only if you want to," she added, squeezing her hand with comfort.

Her two besties had been dealing with her secret crush for too long. It was time to take action. They'd both encouraged her to finally take the leap and approach him, plying her with encouraging quotes about risk, and taking hours to glam up her appearance tonight. Pres tugged nervously at the hem of her black dress and tried to drag in a breath. It was almost impossible with her iron clad, extra tight Spanx and the special push-up bra that cut into her bones. Her feet were squeezed into three-inch-high heels that were hard to walk in, and the little black dress was stretched to its capacity over her voluptuous curves. She couldn't find anything sexy in a size 22 so she'd stuffed her body into the 18 and told herself she'd make it work.

A rush of terror washed over her like a violent tsunami wave, making her question approaching Nolan, a man who made every part of her body hum. Nolan Banks was beautiful. Popular. An athlete who came from a wealthy family. He planned to graduate with a Business Finance degree and join his family's business on Wall Street. Their paths would have rarely crossed, except for her expert stalking tendencies, and the one class that had merged their paths together by her fervent prayers for a sign they were meant to be together.

Creative Writing 200.

It was a senior class, but she'd gotten special approval to take it due to her high grades and the sign-off of her advisor. When she *walked in, she had no idea Nolan would be in the class, and she almost dropped it. Writing was her safe place, and being seated in the same room with the man she crushed on from afar would wreck her concentration. But the temptation of being near to him overruled her head, so Monday, Wednesdays and Fridays were her all-time favorite days of the week.*

His sense of humor, looks, and charisma enamored her. But it was his poet's soul that locked the entire thing up for her. Nolan was perfection. His writing was hauntingly fragile and beautiful—an elegant prose that poked fun at himself—while at the same time allowing his vulnerability to seep through. The class showed her his true heart, and that was when she knew he was meant to be hers—even if he didn't know it yet.

If only she had a shot to prove it to him.

Aubrey shook her blonde mane and grabbed her other hand. "You're daydreaming again. Come on, let's get you hooked up with a drink so you can relax. Then we'll plan your approach."

"Don't leave me," she gulped out, squeezing tight.

Libby smiled with her usual sweetness. "We'd never leave you. It's going to be fine, I promise."

Presley nodded, trying to make herself believe it, and walked with her friends into the party.

CHAPTER 3

"I'M GOING TO THROW UP."

Aubrey Stewart took a sip of champagne and gave her the same look she'd perfected over the years. Patient, yet firm. A combination of ruthless bitch and understanding mother, with a flurry of determined energy that no one was able to resist. "No, you're not. Look at this outfit Trinity sent over. If I swung that way, I'd do you in a heartbeat."

Libby gave her a sympathetic hug and shook out a mint from her purse. "Here, this will help settle your stomach. Aubrey's right—holy shit, girl, you are hot as hell and Nolan Banks will drop to his knees when he catches sight of you."

Presley smiled at the rare curse word her friend threw out for her sake, and felt her heart swell. She prided herself on her reputation as a corporate professional, able to negotiate a contract and command a roomful of men without hesitation. Working in a world that rewarded ruthlessness and worshipped money, any type of emotion was a weakness. She thrived in such an environment and never apologized for who she was. But with Aubrey and Libby, she had nothing she needed to hide and no reason to do so.

Aubrey headed the media division of LWW. Her whirlwind energy, forceful personality, and gorgeous blonde looks had made her a success in both the dating and business world. She still hadn't found the love of her life yet, but she was happily exploring all options and relished every moment of her life. She'd been a role model for Presley in all aspects.

Libby Warren made up the third person in their tight trio. She headed up the not for profit chapter of LWW Enterprises, and ran one of the most successful local charities in the state, The Wish Network, in honor of her brother who had died from spinal bifida. She was only 5'2, with a sweet, helpful demeanor, but everyone learned early she was as strong as steel. If she wanted something, nothing and no one would get in her way. A complete dynamo in the business world, Libby made up the perfect balance of their friendship. She certainly brought a down-to-earth presence and positivity that was needed.

Huddled in her bedroom, her friends were helping her get ready for her drop-in with Nolan. Trinity had sent over the schedule and pegged tomorrow afternoon as the perfect time to pop in and rock his world. Presley figured she could handle it. After all, this wasn't a college party and she wasn't that fat, awkward teen anymore.

Unfortunately, the woman she'd blossomed into sometimes fell back on old memories. She'd tried on the outfit, looked in the mirror, and only spied the humiliation and ugliness of her youth. A quick phone call brought her best friends running to talk her off the literal edge.

She sighed miserably and sat on the edge of the bed. "I'm

sorry, guys. You have better things to do than babysit me. I'm sure I'll be fine."

Both her friends shot her a glare. "Don't insult us," Aubrey said. "Remember our pact after we ditched those three men in Vegas because we thought they were setting us up for a sex kidnapping scheme?"

Libby groaned and stretched out on the king size, lace-quilted bed covered with lilac pillows. Her bedroom was decorated with loud feminine colors and frills with no apology. "You mean the dental salesmen? Oh, my God, so embarrassing. They were attending a conference and just wanted to get laid. I cannot believe we called the police."

Presley lay back beside Libby, propping her head on her elbow. "They spent all night being questioned. I felt terrible."

"We tried to apologize but they ran away," Libby added, half closing her eyes at the memory. "I've never had men afraid of me before."

Aubrey sunk down on the mattress with them, protecting her champagne glass. "Listen, I still think it was a cover story—they were too boring. That creeped me out. No one is that normal at a Vegas bar. Besides, you're missing the point!"

"Which is?" Presley asked.

"We're here for each other whenever. You just call the bat mobile number and we all appear. That's the pact we made, remember?"

"We were kind of drunk," Libby pointed out.

"We were drunk when we decided to start Ladies Who Write, and look how that worked out," Aubrey said.

Presley grinned. "Hell, yeah, you're right. Thanks for being my Robins."

Aubrey frowned. "I'm Catwoman. I love the leather catsuit."

"But she's a villain," Presley said.

"Who cares? She wants to sleep with Batman. I think that inside she's really a heroine. Now, that would make a great book!"

"I want to be Batgirl," Libby cut in. "I like the motorcycle."

"That's cool," Presley said. "I'll stick with Batman since he has the Batmobile. Guys, what if I see Nolan and I get tongue-tied like I used to? Remember when I would panic and just stare because I was too afraid to talk? What if I humiliate myself all over again?"

"You won't," Libby said confidently. "You've run business meetings with scary CEOs and negotiated deals without a sweat. He's just one man. You got this, girl."

"But I'm good with business. I can switch off my brain and excel at that role. I still suck at being a seductress. It just feels awkward. What if I trip? What if I say something stupid? What if he doesn't think I'm attractive?"

Aubrey spoke up. "Pres, you have to reach deep and funnel the Queen Bitch of Seduction and maybe treat Nolan like a business project, a deal you must land. Remember, it's a role. Think it. Live it. Be it. Don't you remember when you lost all the weight and you had to remind yourself every day in the mirror that you were a worthy, beautiful person, on the inside *and* outside?"

She nodded. "Yeah."

Aubrey reached for her hand and squeezed. "Because you are. This is your moment to claim. This is your moment to shine. Remember what he did to you, and strut into that bar of his with your head held high, knowing you are so much better than him. Make him regret ever leaving your life."

Libby grabbed her other hand. "Exactly. Think of all those

books you read and edited when the heroine finally got her revenge. It's simple. Make your entrance. Be cool and distant. Own every bit of this grand meeting with confidence and some sexy, and then leave him wanting every bit of you."

"Show some skin," Aubrey jumped in. "Tell him your name."

"Then wait for the horror and shame that overcomes him," Libby said. "When he stammers out an apology, you shake your head like you barely remember. Give him that stare that makes men wither on the spot. Then you walk out and maybe shake your rear a bit so his eyes widen with greater appreciation."

"His mouth will hang open and he'll be desperate to say more," Aubrey said. "But you won't give him another opportunity. Then, it will finally be done."

The image of that future moment crystallized in front of her.

Finally, she'd be the one to reject him. To hold the power. To prove he didn't break her and never would.

Her friends were right. It was needed to close the chapter on the past.

Her nerves settled. She smiled at her friends and squeezed both of their hands. "Thank you, ladies. I got this."

They nodded as they clinked glasses and chattered about the various, delicious scenarios for the next day.

CHAPTER 4

PRESLEY STARED INTO THE BATHROOM MIRROR AND TRIED desperately to psych herself up to go back to the party.

God, she wanted to go home.

Misery choked her throat, but she took a breath and tried to repair some of the damage to her lipstick. Already, the once creamy stain was now all flaky and dried up. On Aubrey and Libby, the stuff never rubbed off or cracked. It was like her face rejected all forms of products made to make her look better.

Such was her life.

She squared her shoulders, determined to be positive. The night wasn't over yet. Sure, Nolan had been endlessly surrounded by his track buddies and a revolving line of hot girls. He didn't have a girlfriend though, and at this point, she just wanted to talk to him. Even a few minutes. To bask in his smile, or share a few seconds of dialogue would be everything. She already had her conversation starter—their last assignment in Creative Writing class. They had to write about a *memory that caused everything to change. Professor Castle demanded raw honesty and nakedness, threatening if it sounded in any way false that he'd give out a failing grade.*

Turning on the faucet to wet her hands, she slid them down her hair to try and take away the frizz. She couldn't let Aubrey and Libby down. She'd promised to be brave.

Just this once.

Like the heroines in her books. Even if they failed, they grew character. They may have been afraid, but not trying caused more regret than taking the safe road.

Suddenly, there was a crash outside.

The bathroom door burst open, and a guy came staggering in, his hands clutching his stomach. She lurched back, her butt hitting the edge of the sink. He reeked of smoke and alcohol. "Hey ya, bubby, I gotta get in and go."

"What?" she asked hesitantly, wondering if she could try to move past him without making contact. "I'm sorry, are you okay?"

He pointed to the toilet, swaying back and forth, as if trying to get there but unable to actually move. "I said hiya gotta get in go!"

"Okay, Romeo, let's get you to the toilet so you can purge. Aww, hell, did he break down the door?"

Presley froze at the familiar drawl of a voice that prickled her nerve endings.

Nolan.

His ocean blue eyes were full of concern, and a slight frown creased his brow. Curly, oaky-brown locks fell messily across his forehead and covered his ears. God, he was tall, towering in the doorway and shrinking the bathroom to the size of a postage stamp. He wore a black t-shirt that stretched tight over his chest. Why did he smell like fresh clean laundry and beach breezes? Most of the guys in college reeked of dirty socks and stale beer. Was it his cologne or did he not sweat like other humans? No, she'd seen him after a track meet, skin damp, hair slick with sweat, breathing heavily as he hurled himself past the 1500 mark ahead of everyone else. Wait—what had he asked?

Heat flushed her. "Huh?"

"Are you okay? I hope he didn't barge in on you. I knew he was going to hurl but I figured he'd go to the bathroom downstairs."

"No! I'm okay, really. He just surprised me."

The guy must've had enough of the conversation, because he tore away from Nolan's grip and lurched across the floor toward the toilet. Then let it rip.

Nolan shook his head. "I knew he shouldn't have done the shots. Oh, here, you probably want to leave."

He grinned, moving away from the doorway, and Presley heard the strains of a symphony in her head, drowning out the sounds of sickness behind her. Was she drunk? Dizzy? Or just mesmerized by that crooked, sexy smile that made her feel he was letting her in on a secret? She stood still and smiled back, refusing to move.

That frown again. "Hey, you sure you're okay? Are you drunk? You should be careful at these parties if you're alone. Do you have friends with you?"

Oh, my God, he was so sweet. He was worried about her! "Yes! I mean . . . no, I'm not drunk, and . . . yes, my friends are here. They're just busy so I figured I'd refresh my lipstick and get some time alone to think a bit."

He cocked his head and studied her. "What are you thinking about in a bathroom during a frat party?"

She blinked. Had she said that? Crap. "Umm, stuff. About life."

More retching. He raised his voice. "Carl, you okay over there?" Presley glanced back and caught a thumbs up signal. "K, buddy, tell me when you're done." He swiveled his gaze back to her. He squinted with curiosity as he stared. She noticed a tiny scar see sawing through his left brow. Fascinating. She wondered how he got it. "So, what type of life things?"

Uh, oh. She was so dumb. Why hadn't she learned to flirt and giggle and do girly things that attracted guys? Instead, she just blurted out anything on her mind. Damn, she couldn't tell him she was obsessing over him. Presley gave a shrug and lied. "Nothing important. Just stuff like what I'll do for my career and where I'll live and if I'll be happy."

His grin widened. "Deep shit. I like it." He studied her face and she stared back, caught up in a trance from his picture-perfect male beauty. His jaw was perfectly squared and his lips perfectly defined. Kind of like a sculpture masterpiece. "Hey, you're in my writing class!"

Pleasure flushed through her. Dear Lord, he remembered! She nodded and tried to act cool. "Yeah."

"What do you think of—"

He was interrupted by a crash, as his friend knocked over the tissue box and swiped at his mouth. Nolan walked past her, grabbing Carl by the elbow. "You feel better, dude?"

"Yasss."

"Good, why don't you lay down and I'll get you some water?" Nolan shot her an apologetic look. "I'm going to walk him next door so he can rest."

"I can bring him some water," she suggested.

"Will you? Thanks, that'll be great."

Heart pounding, she raced back into the kitchen and checked the refrigerator for bottled water. Grabbing one from the back, she gulped for breath and tried to calm herself down. Finally, she was getting her

THE CHARM OF YOU

opportunity to talk to him. She needed to make sure she was calm, witty, funny, and flirty. No more stupid rambling.

She dragged in a breath, mentally channeling the strong-minded, sexy heroines in her romance novels, and swore she'd be the woman Nolan Banks couldn't forget.

CHAPTER 5

NOLAN SWUNG THE LAST BOX ON TOP OF THE BAR AND WIPED HIS forehead. Almost done. The past two weeks he'd been working nonstop to hit his opening day target, and now he'd be able to put the date in ink.

His gaze swept over his surroundings. The small pub had been run down and kept open for only the hard drinkers in need of a cheap whiskey and a listening ear. When the owner took off for bigger glories and put it up for sale for practically a gift, Nolan knew it was time to make the move. He bought the property, hired a lawyer, and expanded to include a small brewery so he could begin making his own beer.

Finally, he was living the dream.

His dream.

One of the best parts?

His brother hadn't even known until the deal was done.

As if conjured up by the power of his thoughts, the bell jingled. Carter Banks crashed through the door, marched up to the bar, and slammed down a piece of paper. "You had the balls to pin this up on my door?" he growled, his meaty fist clenching.

Nolan tried to keep the smug grin from his face and glanced down at the flyer. "What's the matter? You don't like it?"

The flyer was his own personal joke finally trumping his big brother. The heading screamed: **No Need to Settle for Quarters – The Bank is Now Open! The First Microbrewery in Port Hudson – Drink YOUR Way!**

The picture showed a palm holding a lonely quarter on the left side, and a bank full of beer on the right.

Carter glared. "You think you're hot shit now, *little brother*? Just remember I've been here longer and I can sway the crowds. People like coming to Quarters. My pub is comfortable and familiar. They may not like your fancy city beer and bite-sized overpriced food."

"Perhaps. Or maybe they've been waiting for something fresh and new. You worried about a little competition?"

Carter let out a short laugh. His blue eyes gleamed with challenge. "Bring it." He shook his head. "Why the hell did you follow me to Port Hudson? For God's sakes, you could've opened up your place in the city or Westchester—not a small college town."

Nolan leaned against the bar and quirked a brow. "I'm the one who went to school here, dude. I'm the one who told you I wanted to open up a bar and name it Quarters in my old college town. How do you think I felt when I was trapped with Mom and Dad on Wall Street and heard you were leaving the business to open up your pub? That you stole my idea, my place, and my name?"

"Bullshit! It was *my* idea! I knew this was the perfect town for a pub when I came to visit you at Boyer University. And I clearly remember claiming the name when we got drunk the night before Thanksgiving. Remember?"

The memory was murky. They'd hunkered down at Sampson's Place for a few drinks that had ended up being an all night binge. And they'd played . . . Quarters. Hmmm . . . "All I remember is Mom flipping out when we were too sick to eat the turkey dinner she actually tried to cook."

Carter winced. "Yeah, she was pissed. But maybe it's best. Mom's cooking is seriously harmful."

"Agreed. But I still maintain you stole my idea."

His brother rolled his eyes. "Dramatic, much? I thought you liked finance. You were always better at it than I was. Dad said you were a natural."

It was the edge in his brother's voice that sucked away Nolan's temper. Carter had been the first to graduate and join the family firm, and it was obvious he'd been miserable. He'd done his time and tried his best while Nolan finished up his degree, but every time Nolan saw his big brother, more zest had seeped out of him. His big announcement of moving to open a bar had shocked them all, but eventually they'd rallied in support for Carter.

Unfortunately, it meant his parents' gaze turned to Nolan after graduation.

"Mom and Dad were proud of you," Nolan told him. "You stuck it out for as long as possible, but you were miserable. At least you could blame leaving on your sucky investments and lack of skill. It was harder for me."

Carter laughed. "You are so messed up. How the hell was it harder for you? You were the golden boy. Athletic star on scholarship. Top honors in college. Corner office after a year on Wall

Street. The Midas touch with stocks. Everyone fucking revered you."

Nolan nodded. "Exactly. It was harder to leave while being on top. Mom and Dad didn't take it well at all. Kept begging me to give it another year. Made me feel like shit, like I had failed them because I didn't want the life they paved for me. Remember those pictures you used to send me?"

His brother liked to send him pics of crowds raising their glasses in salute at Quarters. Carter lounged behind the bar, in jeans and a comfy t-shirt, his face wreathed with a shit-eating grin like a king in his own castle. Nolan used to stare at them, his body contained in his expensive, custom suit, his freedom constricted by the huge mahogany desk with endless monitors perched in front of him. Day after day, he'd fantasized about leaving New York's financial district—the lure of endless riches and blood-thirsty mental games that rewarded only the shrewdest. How long had Nolan tried to be the son they always wanted, especially after Carter took off? How long had he ached for the day he allowed himself to follow his own dream?

Too long.

Carter regarded him curiously. "Yeah."

"Every time I looked at those pictures, I realized you'd been brave enough to create your own path, on your terms. And if you could do it, I knew I could. I never thanked you for that, for showing me what I was missing."

A short silence settled between them, full of unspoken emotion, acceptance and the bond of blood that pumped through their veins. Fighting with Carter was part of the seams of his life, but underneath all the shit, lay a treasure of brotherly love and trust that no one could break. To Nolan, family was everything, and that was another reason he'd chosen Port Hudson, even though he'd never admit it to Carter.

His brother cleared his throat. "Okay."

Nolan grinned. "Okay."

"Maybe Landon will do what we couldn't. She seems happy."

His poor parents had somehow produced two boys interested in drinking and food rather than running a finance empire. Thank God, they had his sister to focus on. Landon may be the youngest, but she seemed to have inherited the genes for Wall Street. A computer genius who was more ruthless than any of them, Landon was slowly building her reputation. "Yeah, she'll probably be the one to save us all. Want a beer? I've got a new batch I just bottled."

Carter shook his head. "Wish I could, but gotta get set up for the dinner rush. Next time."

"Sounds good."

Carter patted his shoulder, then lumbered toward the door.

Nolan held his breath, wondering if he'd see it.

He did.

The sign for The Bank held a single quarter hanging pathetically in the logo.

His brother whipped around and shook his fist in the air, his usual gesture when words and insults wouldn't do.

"Like the sign?" Nolan asked cheerfully.

"You're such a dick," his brother finally gritted out. "Wait till I hold an epic Happy Hour on your opening night."

The bell jingled and the door slammed behind him.

Nolan laughed with the sweet sing of adrenaline in his blood that always occurred after fighting with his brother. God, he'd missed the guy.

He took a moment in the quiet to look around and take

stock. The restored oak bar shone with a dull gleam, and the glass wall behind filled with much more than whiskey. The drafts were plentiful and varied, including three of his own private brews he'd been perfecting in NYC. He'd been smart enough to hook up with a mentor to learn the business from the ground up, and began crafting his own formulas until he felt solid enough to go on his own. He'd invested in a bottling machine and some efficient equipment so he could begin selling locally.

The pub itself was inviting and offered something unique. A scattering of comfortable red booths and high-topped tables were limited, as was the menu. He sure as hell didn't intend to compete with the local restaurants—including his brother's—preferring to find his niche with original bar bites paired with unique brews for late lunches and fun evenings. The rest of the space was dedicated to beer tasting and an array of games to include a pinball machine, pool table, and several dart boards. He had a juke box and air hockey table on order.

Nolan looked at his running list of to-do items. He had a million tasks to complete, but he allowed the surge of pride and contentment to hit full force. He finally had his own bar and brewery. His life. His terms. Hard work never scared him, and the challenge of making The Bank a success called to his consistent sense of challenge.

The staff had been hired and would be here in a few days to start training. His chef cost a fortune and was stolen from Tom Collichio's restaurant in NYC, and worth every penny. Mick had created a special tasting menu for each individual craft beer. Nolan was about to launch something that had never been done before in the area. A gourmet pub experience on par with a five-star restaurant. Nolan just hoped his chef could deal with living in a college town when he was used to the grittiness and glitz of the city.

He grabbed a box cutter, slit open the top, and launched into the classic, *Whistle While You Work* in isolated glory.

"Do you do karaoke, also?" a husky, amused voice interrupted.

He swung a startled gaze toward the door, realizing the bell hadn't gone off.

Then stared.

Holy shit.

The woman standing before him was so perfect, he figured she wasn't real. Blinking hard, he studied her from her head to her toes, then back up again, his tongue sticking to the roof of his mouth like he'd just downed a jar of peanut butter.

She was all ripe curves and lush roundness, the original Eve reincarnated to drive men back to their primate selves. Her hair was a vibrant burgundy, the thick, shiny strands pin straight and falling just to the top of her shoulders. The side shaggy bangs emphasized the gorgeous elegance to her face—the high cheekbones, pert nose, sharp chin, and a heart-shaped mouth, painted a delicious shade of red, and pursed in obvious amusement. Her eyes were huge on her face and expressive, windows to her soul and maybe his. Their color of a summer storm—misty gray with a touch of blue—added a depth and intensity that threw him off balance. She stood with perfect ease, allowing him to look his fill, hands rested on her hips. The white wrap-around dress was a soft, clingy material that hugged every curve, cutting low in the front that emphasized ripe breasts and the pale valley of white skin between. The edge of white lace on her shoulder teased him, making him long to see if her bra and panties were also virginal white and what deliciousness they hid. Her shoes were sinful red, with a spiked heel and open in the front to flash cherry red toenails.

He'd seen gorgeous women before. Hell, he'd dated many of them, and took the majority to bed. But something about her slammed through him like a recognition and poignant memory, driving him to reach out and touch her.

"You done?"

He shook his head, trying to clear his throat, and fought the warmth heating his cheeks. "Uh, yeah, sorry. You surprised me."

She flashed a grin, and walked toward him with deliberate intention, hips swinging generously. His gaze got stuck on another peek of white lace as her dress flapped open, then closed around her thighs. Was she wearing stockings and garters? Did women even own those anymore? At that moment, he'd pay a billion dollars to find out.

The blood from his thinking head drained to his now bulging head below, and he gripped the edge of the bar for balance.

She leaned forward, regarding him with deliberate precision. "You're new."

His breath stuttered as he gazed into her eyes, caught up in the swirls of blue and silver. A sense of déjà vu fell over him, as if he'd done the same exact thing before, but the memory skittered away before he was able to grasp it. Thank God she wasn't wearing a ring or he may have burst into silly tears. "You're hot."

A husky laugh escaped her lips. "I know."

He grinned back, utterly charmed. "Welcome to the Bank. I'm Nolan Banks."

One brow arched. "Clever. You've done great things with the place." Her gaze swept over the bar and around the room, taking it all in. A rush of pride surged that he was finally able to say he owned something he believed in. "When do you open?"

"About a month. Soft launch in two weeks. Saturday night."

"I heard you'll have a selection of craft beer you make yourself."

"You heard right," he said. "I expanded through the back and installed a brewery section. You like beer?"

"Who doesn't?"

He leaned forward, fascinated. "You seem more like the wine and champagne type."

She waved a hand in dismissal. "I adore a good Dom Pérignon and Rosé, but I can appreciate a cold brew on a hot day."

"Who are you and what do I have to do to see you again?"

She ignored the question and emitted a delicate snort. "Why did you decide to open in Port Hudson?"

He scratched his chin. "You're nosy. When do I get to ask questions?"

"When I feel like answering."

She talked to him like she was used to giving orders and being obeyed. The thought only intrigued him more. "I went to school here. Headed to the city to make a name for myself, and realized my heart never left this place. Decided to open my own business and see if I can make it work here. Do you live in town? What do you do?"

Her gaze narrowed, as if his last response was important. "What's so great about this town that your heart couldn't forget?"

He never even thought about lying. "This was the only place I ever felt truly like myself."

Was that a flash of disappointment in her eyes or was he

nuts? There was something going on here he couldn't seem to grasp—something important he didn't want to screw up. "Do I know you?" he asked.

She hesitated, then let out a soft sigh. "It doesn't matter. I have to go."

"Wait!"

She didn't listen. Just pivoted on her heel and presented him with the most luscious, gorgeous ass he'd ever seen. "Do you want to be my date for the soft launch opening?"

She stopped and turned halfway. Tilted her head, as if to consider. Those juicy apple red lips pursed. "You don't even know my name."

"You're right. What's your name?"

She paused. The air squeezed with a slight tension, and Nolan sensed she was preparing for a big announcement. He held his breath, waiting. "Presley."

The name sang in his brain like a song. His tongue tingled, as if craving to say it aloud. "Wanna be my date for the soft launch opening, *Presley*?"

Her gaze dove deep, searching for something he didn't know how to give. Seconds passed. He said nothing, waiting her out, and the oddest flash of pain flickered over her face before it was quickly masked. But that couldn't be. He didn't know her. It must've been a trick of the light as he wouldn't forget the gorgeous goddess standing before him.

"Do you ask every woman who walks into your bar for a date?" she asked curiously.

"Nope. Only you."

"But you haven't even opened yet. Plus, I only date men who are worthy of me."

Oh, she was absolutely delicious. She practically stuck her

nose up in the air at the idea of just saying yes to him. When was the last time a woman had bothered to even tell him *no*? Or maybe? Hell, she was about to walk out on him like he'd failed her on all counts and wouldn't measure up to her. He'd never been so intrigued by a woman.

Growing up terribly spoiled, it'd been too easy to get any woman he desired, until he wondered if he was just a shallow prick who couldn't manage to see past his own need for a challenge. But he'd never experienced this type of heat in his blood or the itch under his skin. "How do you deem a man worthy?"

She practically sneered. Her eyes turned to steel gray and sparked with a fierce heat that seared him like a flame. "It'd be nice if he remembered me."

Nolan blinked. "A man would have to be dead to forget you."

She threw back her head and laughed. The sound was a like a throaty growl that was sexier than the purr of a Maserati engine. "I wish. See ya around, Nolan Banks. Good luck with your beer."

He opened his mouth to call for her again, but it was too late. The bell tinkled merrily and the door swooshed behind her, leaving the bar in silence. She left him wanting more. He just wasn't exactly sure what *more* entailed. Yet.

Presley.

Oh, they'd be seeing each other again. There was no way that woman was walking out of his bar and out of his life before he did everything in his power to convince her he was worthy. He had plenty of people who could help find her and give him all the important details.

Nolan grabbed his phone and got to work.

CHAPTER 6

WEAVING HER WAY THROUGH THE CROWDS, PRESLEY CLIMBED THE stairs and knocked on the door next to the bedroom.

"Come in."

She pushed it open. "Here you go," she said, handing him the bottle and praying her fingers weren't shaking.

"Thanks." Carl was half passed out on the bed, his feet hanging over the edge. "Dude, drink some water, you'll feel better." He forced his friend to drink as he could stand, then swung his legs on the mattress and took off his shoes. Carl grunted, rolled over, and let out a loud fart.

Nolan shot her a look.

They both burst into laughter.

"Sorry about this. Hope we didn't ruin your night."

She shook her head hard. "No, other than my girlfriends, I don't know too many people here. I'm only a sophomore."

"Wow, that means you must be pretty smart to be in Professor

Castle's class. He's tough and it's usually reserved for juniors and seniors."

"I always liked to write," she said. "Actually, I'm even better at fixing other people's stuff. It's like I have this tunnel vision of exactly what needs to be done to make a story better. Sometimes, it's a pain when I'm trying to enjoy reading a book and my brain is jumping around telling the author how to tweak."

"Wish I had that problem. English is my worst subject."

She shifted her weight and gazed at him shyly. "That can't be true. I heard your last piece in class. It was really good."

He jerked back in surprise. "You think? He said it was staged and dramatic."

She reached out and touched his arm. Her fingertips tingled at the delicious feel of hair-roughened muscles. "The first part was a bit contrived, but the final half was brilliant. I loved the way you described how easy everything comes to you—running, grades, friends. The way it makes you wonder if you're gifted or just a fraud, worrying when the day will be it all goes away. It was real and that's what made it more moving."

He cocked his head. Those gorgeous curls flopped over one eye. "Makes me sound like an arrogant ass," he muttered, looking adorably embarrassed.

"No, it makes you honest," she retorted, chin tilted up so she could gaze up at him.

He smiled, and she smiled back, and in that moment, everything was perfect. He was perfect.

"What's your name again?"

"Presley."

"I'm Nolan."

She laughed. "I know."

"Oh, sorry, to be honest, I'm terrible at names. I forget all the time."

Silence enveloped them. She realized she was still gripping his arm, and slowly released her fingers. Her heart thundered and sweat prickled under her arms. She searched desperately for something else to say, but already knew he was ready to dismiss her and move on. She'd have to be content with their brief conversation. Maybe he'd remember her when he saw her in class now. Maybe—

"Want to get a drink?" he asked.

She blinked. "Huh?"

"A drink. Water if you want, of course. Unless you want to go check on your friends?"

"No! No, I mean, my friends are fine. And I do drink so let's go grab something."

He shot her an amused glance. "Good to know. Carl needs to sleep it off. Let's go."

Presley followed him out of the bedroom, her head spinning in pure joy.

CHAPTER 7

WHAT THE FUCK? THE BASTARD DIDN'T EVEN REMEMBER HER? HAD she changed that much? Or was she just not that memorable to the Great Nolan?

Presley broke into a litany of all the curse words in her arsenal as she walked furiously down the street. She'd planned the first meeting perfectly, choosing to take Trinity's advice. Play it cool, but give him just enough rope to yank it tightly if he jumped.

Oh, yeah, he'd jumped alright like he wanted to jump her. Practically drooled on the bar's gleaming counter and made his interest well known. Hell, he'd asked her out after a five-minute conversation so her ploy had worked.

Unfortunately, one important thing had blown up with the plan.

She'd stupidly assumed he'd remember her. They'd gone to college together. Slept together. Been in English class together. She'd fantasized about their reunion scene over and over in her

THE CHARM OF YOU

mind, until long after dawn, and he didn't even know who she was and that stung a bit.

Her fantasy played out like this: Her badass entrance. His intrigue and flirty demeanor. His shock after hearing her name and finally recognizing who she was. His dawning realization of their past. The discomfort and endless apologies spilling from his lips for the way he completely humiliated her. Hell, she'd even practiced the gestures in the mirror. The roll of her eyes and wave of her hand in pure dismissal. The cold flicker of her gaze as she dismissed him, and confided she barely even remembered him anyway. It was to be her greatest moment of revenge. The complete rejection of Nolan Banks.

Instead, he'd gazed into her eyes, heard her name, and registered . . . nothing.

The mid-afternoon sun shone bright and hot. Crowds littered Main Street with people going about their days as they grabbed late lunches, and lounged on benches while sipping lattes, reading books, and chatting with friends and neighbors. She passed the Paws Café where leashed canines feasted on treats and lapped up bowls of crystal clear water while their owners ate proper lunches at café tables, heads bent over their phones. The beauty of Port Hudson always made her pause, reminding her of why they'd decided to build the LWW Head-quarters here.

The sweep of the jagged rock crashing against the blue-gray water of the Hudson. The melding of sharp Manhattan business executives joining quirky, creative artists. College students mixing with groups of millennials, Generation X, and Baby Boomers. The town was a melting pot of everything she loved and believed in the world.

But not today.

Today, there was nothing but shame burning and raging through her body. She'd lost her virginity and her heart to a man who'd forgotten her. This was so much worse than she imagined. She hadn't even been important enough to remember. She was a piece of dust floating in his vision. A smooshed bug on his windshield. The black smudge of scum on the heel of his shoe.

The endless metaphors rolled through her mind, some of them so good she made a note to write them down for future use. Writers were always searching for various descriptive metaphors, and she despised a cliché like any other publisher. Too bad the genius was at her expense.

A wave of depression pressed down on her, and the old feelings of inadequacy threatened. She wasn't ready to go back to the office—not like this. She needed a boost, a shot of something positive to make this negative day feel better. A reminder of who she really was—not the false image her younger self saw when she looked in the mirror.

Presley made a quick detour, her heels tapping against the crooked pavement. The cheerful sunflower yellow sign lit like a beacon over the red brick building, and she pushed open the door, drawing in a deep breath. The scent of paper, vanilla, and freedom hit her like a drug, buzzing in her veins. Rummaging for her phone, she tapped out a quick text as she walked to the back of the Nook 'n Crannies bookstore.

Got a minute to talk? I saw him.

Immediately, the *** floated on her screen. *Yes, where r u?*

Bookstore.

Be there in five.

Presley smiled and slid her phone back in her bag. She spent the next few minutes browsing the shelves, losing herself in the world of imagination that had saved her life many times in her past. In the world of books, anything could happen. Book boyfriends were the best. Injustices were addressed and righted. Heartbreak was healed. Love stories ended happily. Even in tragedy, the pages were filled with words that addressed one of the most important themes in her life.

Hope. There was always hope. God knows, many mornings she'd needed to believe in such a message when she rolled out of bed and was forced to confront the day. Now, she'd made a career on giving the world the best stories of which she was capable. Her stable of writers were legendary, and the ones she culled from the slush pile were some of her best. She ran LWW Publications differently than traditional publishers. She embraced Indie publishing, feeling the market and creative reign only strengthened the creative soul, and had no problem adjusting price and playing with sales on a regular basis. She concentrated on backlist rather than just front list, and offered an author more of a career than a chance to publish one book. Writer's Digest had ranked LWW as one of the top publishers authors wanted to sign with, and she'd been featured at multiple conferences all over the world.

Books had given her everything.

Now, she gave back.

The scent of exotic sandalwood and citrus hit her nostrils the same time her friend tugged on her wrist. She turned.

Aubrey faced her with a fierce frown, her golden eyes flashing with concern. "Are you okay?" she demanded.

"No. Yes. I don't know," she said.

"Did you call Libby?"

"No, she's at a special charity event today in recognition of her brother. I didn't want to disturb her."

"Got it. We'll catch her up with things later. Come on."

Aubrey snagged her hand and led her to the back of the bookstore, through the connecting door, and into the attached café. The reverted bedroom now provided a cozy space to drink coffee, read books, and chill. Eclectic music spilled from the speakers from Sinatra to Radiohead and everything in between. Apple green sofas, mismatched chairs and tables, and the scent of serious caffeine drifted in the air. "Darlene, we need two skinny vanilla lattes with double shots, please," Aubrey called out to the barista, a young college student with waist length red hair and various piercings. "And we'll split a chocolate chip scone."

"Got it," Darlene called back.

Presley fell into the comfy plaid oversized chair and buried her face in her hands. "How'd you know I needed chocolate?" she asked pitifully.

Aubrey patted her hand. "Because I know you, babe. You never send out an SOS unless it's serious. Did he say something to upset you? Was he an ass? I swear to God, if he was, I'll make it my personal mission to ruin him."

A choked laugh escaped. "No, it was the opposite. His jaw dropped the moment I walked in and he was all up in my space, looking like at me like I was his territory and he was planning an intimate invasion. Even asked me to his soft launch opening in two weeks."

Aubrey nodded smugly. "Knew it. You're like sex on a stick today. Trinity has mad talent picking the perfect prey-picking outfit. It sounds like he was definitely the predator. Okay, so what happened when he recognized you? Did he freak? Was he so embarrassed he got defensive? Please tell me he at least apologized."

Presley stared into her friend's eyes. "He didn't even remember me."

Darlene walked over, handing them their coffee and the scone neatly split in half. Aubrey shook her head as if trying to clear it. "Wait, I don't understand. What do you mean? Did you tell him your name? I mean, you look completely different, Pres, so maybe he was a bit slow on the take?"

She grabbed her scone and took a big bite, letting the wash of sugar stream into her blood and give her hope the day would get better. God, it was good. She was careful of her calories and lived a healthy lifestyle, but baked goods were her drug of choice. "Aubrey, he had no clue who I was. He looked into my eyes, heard my name, and there was zero recognition. I was just some random hot chick he wanted to pick up in his new bar."

Her friend blinked and took a few big gulps of coffee. "Holy crapola. Are you sure he wasn't pretending not to recognize you?"

"Trust me—he had no idea we even slept together. Oh, my God, what does that say about me, Aubrey? The man I gave my virginity to forgot about the whole damn thing! It obviously wasn't special for him like it was for me. Jeez."

"Breathe, babe. Let me think about this a moment."

Taking Aubrey's advice, Presley took some deep breaths in between finishing her scone, and knew her friend would come up with the perfect remark to soothe her. She always did. Suddenly, Aubrey's golden eyes took on a ruthless gleam that shot shivers down her spine.

"He doesn't remember you? Fine. We'll use the knowledge to bury him."

"What do you mean? We can't kill him and I already told Trinity I refused to call Jack."

Aubrey's brow rose in interest. "Jack still does that type of side work? Good to know."

"I don't want to maim him either!"

"We're going to do worse. We'll hit him where most men feel the pain the most."

"I can't get to his heart, Aubrey. He doesn't even know me!"

"Not his heart, babe. Think bigger."

Finally, it dawned on her. Presley's eyes widened. "His dick?"

"Bingo. He wants you. He thinks you're a hot piece. Great. You're going to lead him on a merry chase through hell. Remember the movie, *How to Lose a Guy in Ten Days*?"

"Of course. That movie is epic."

"That's your Bible but we're giving it a twist. You're going to make him fall for you by becoming his perfect woman, but instead of trying to get him to dump you in ten days, you get him to fall in love. Then *you* dump *his* ass."

"You're kidding."

"Nope. Use your body and that sharp mind as a weapon. Make him crazy to sleep with you and win you, as that man probably loves a good challenge. When he begins to fall hard, you yank the ground from underneath and watch him fall into the hole."

The idea hit her full force, bringing back her original fantasy of revenge. Was it possible? Could she pull off such a coup? "I don't know. How often does a man forget he has sex with a woman? I must've sucked in bed big time or he's bagged so many women that I'm a blur."

Aubrey rolled her eyes. "Are you kidding me? He was the one who sucked in bed, remember! You may have been crushing on him hard, but he pretty much stuck it in you, got off, and rolled over. This man is a dud—not a stud. He deserves to be exposed!"

She couldn't help the laugh that escaped her lips. Her friend always knew how to put the perfect spin on things. "I'm not really a sexpot. I was able to pull off the role for a few minutes, but I don't know if I'm capable of giving him a good chase. Not like Kate Hudson. Maybe we should get Becca to seduce him," she said glumly. "She'd take care of him good."

Becca was Aubrey's assistant. Besides being ruthless with organization, she was a well-known man eater. Men followed her around like helpless puppies, and if she deigned to take one to bed, he rarely saw her bedroom again. She was gorgeous, confident, and everything Presley always wanted to be.

Aubrey waved her suggestion away. "No, this is personal. You're the one who has to do it. Pres, you've changed. You run a billion-dollar company. You're healthy, sexy and so damn smart. This is your time now, and I won't let you walk away. Make him pay. Do it for every woman who's been slept with and forgotten. Do it for our gender."

The passionate words touched something deep inside and set off an explosion of emotion. Aubrey was right. She refused to sneak around, feeling shameful for a jerk who didn't even remember how badly he'd hurt her. He'd proved he didn't care what was beneath the surface—he only catered to the beautiful people. Just because she'd been overweight and awkward, he'd judged her unworthy.

It was time to do what a good book would accomplish.

Be the bold heroine. Bring her own brand of justice. And kick all the ass.

"You're right," she said. "I'm tired of letting him get away with what he did. I can do this. I can turn myself into the perfect woman and break him."

"That's my girl!" They high-fived and grinned at each other in triumph. "Now, you work better with a plan in place so let's put one together. Strategy. Outfits. We'll get Libby up to speed and Trinity on wardrobe. She'll need to bring Cam in on this one and have a hotline in place if you need any of us. Let's get to work."

Aubrey pulled out her planner, her LWW custom pen, and turned to a fresh blank page.

Presley blinked away tears. "You're the best, Aubrey. I love you."

"Love you, too. Now, let's get ready to kick some male ass."

CHAPTER 8

NOLAN WALKED INTO LWW ENTERPRISES AND TOOK IN THE exquisite detail of the building with admiration. His family was born and bred for New York City streets, and he'd seen both the grace and vulgarity of money and how people use it. He hadn't been surprised to learn that Presley Cabot was a billionaire and the head of one of the most powerful companies in the US. Everything about the woman screamed savvy and confident. What surprised him was her choices.

She'd chosen to build the headquarters in the small town of Port Hudson, a place more known for its college university than a business-focused area with big money. The move had guaranteed an uptick in the economy, including the demand for more housing for its employees. He didn't understand why she didn't rent a swanky place in Manhattan where she'd be in the center of the action with big companies and could show off her wealth.

The second surprise was how she'd structured her company.

From the moment he entered the property protected by thick green tress and lush lawns, he noticed the solar panels and sleek glass structure that seemed built to collect the most natural light. Signs proudly boasted it was one of the greenest buildings in the world, built to spec with renewable materials and the ability to re-use waste and rainwater. The design was elegant but open, welcome but professional—a perfect blending of business and familiarity that welcomed customers and employees.

Nolan had seen a hell of a lot of architecture and he was damn impressed. This woman continued to impress him from her beautiful looks, to her bold demeanor, to her business shrewdness.

Presley Cabot just kept getting more and more intriguing.

The elevator dinged for the twentieth floor. He stepped onto gleaming marble floors and walked to the receptionist desk that was its own work of art—shaped like a giant S and carved in rich walnut. Framed magazine posters and book covers covered the champagne-colored walls. A giant, glittering black chandelier was the focal point, and an array of chairs and couches in artistic gold and black flowers scattered in the waiting area. Presley's office was an extension of her: elegant and enticing.

"May I help you, sir?"

He smiled at the woman behind the desk. With her golden curls, bright smile, and sleek black dress, she seemed the perfect face for LWW Enterprises. "Yes, I have an appointment to see Presley Cabot. Noon."

"Ah, yes, Mr. Peterson? We're thrilled you're in town. Can I get you anything? Coffee, water?"

"No, thank you."

"Very well, then, come with me, Ms. Cabot is ready for you."

"Thank you." He straightened up, pulling down the sleeves of his charcoal sport coat, as he followed her down the hall in his comfortable jeans. He'd decided when he left Wall Street he'd never wear a tie again. Not even to a wedding. Nothing was going to strangle his breath or freedom again.

The woman pushed open the heavily carved door. "Mr. Peterson," she announced.

He didn't hesitate as he walked into her office and the receptionist shut the door behind him.

A bit smug at his easy success, Nolan took confident strides forward, ready to show her he was a worthy opponent.

Until he stopped cold.

And stared dumbly at the sight before him that nearly took his breath away and knocked him on his knees.

Because there she was, behind a big-ass, sprawling desk fit for a Queen, lounging in the red leather chair with her gorgeous legs propped up on the desk. Her feet were clad in the sexiest, fuck-me heels, completely nude with a peekaboo toe and multiple straps winding around her ankle, snaking up her calf. He blinked, his gaze stuck on those perfect, long and bare legs, then dragged his eyes up to her exposed thighs where the hem of her bright yellow skirt stopped his trip to heaven. The fabric was slinky and clung to her curvy hips, then draped in the front with the sole attempt to show off her impressive cleavage. A golden locket nestled between her lush breasts, which might as well been a bullseye, targeting him, teasing him with every breath.

After ogling the stunning woman with pin-up model curves, his gaze finally traveled upward as it slammed into heather grey eyes full of wicked intent, leaving his mouth desert-dry and his dick rock-hard.

No woman has ever had such an effect on him. He wanted to claim her before he'd even touched her.

Presley slicked her tongue over juicy, red lips and raised one arched brow. "Hmm, funny. You don't look like Mr. Peterson— the head of Voltage Publications. Unless you've done a Benjamin Button and reversed your age by thirty years."

Son-of-a-bitch. She'd known all along he'd lied about his identity in order to secure this appointment. Admiration flowed through him, along with a strange punch in his gut that urged him closer. The spicy scent of orange blossoms and clove filled the air, making him want to breathe deeper. "How did you know?" he asked, stopping on the opposite side of the monstrous espresso structure that held two oversized monitors, dozens of papers, and a toppling pile of books. "I thought I covered my tracks nicely."

She gave a half shrug and reached for her Starbucks cup, seemingly already bored with his conversation. "You're predictable."

Male pride stung, he still couldn't help laughing. Why did he have to be attracted to a woman who gave him shit? It would be so much easier to find a more willing partner for an affair. Unfortunately, Nolan knew it was way too late for him. He was officially smitten by this woman who challenged his mind and teased him with her luscious curves. "Then I'll have to up my game."

Another shrug. "Maybe you have no game left." She sipped her coffee and studied him, those stunning eyes shielding her secrets. He ached to know every detail about this woman, but knew he'd have his work cut out for him.

THE CHARM OF YOU

"Come to lunch with me and find out."

She tilted her head. Tapped her index finger again those bee-stung lips as if considering. "Why?"

Her question delighted him. "Because the moment you walked into my brewery, I haven't been able to get you off my mind."

"How sweet." She fluttered her lashes. "Too bad I forgot you the moment I walked out of your brewery."

He dropped into the chair opposite the massive desk and hooked his foot over his knee. He made no attempt to hide his naked admiration for those amazing legs or the brazen way she challenged him to go and try. Her foot flexed, lifting the spiked heel, and those sleek muscles clenched under golden skin. His dick practically wept and got strangled in his jeans. "Ouch. What if I confessed you were the first woman in a long while to intrigue me?"

"Yeah? What intrigues you so much?"

He warmed up to the topic. "Besides your quick wit and superior intelligence? Your eyes. When I look into your eyes, I seem to lose track of time. I don't want to be anywhere else."

Did she actually look *bored* with his compliment? She gave a long-suffering sigh, regarding him like he was mentally challenged. "Please tell me you have better things in your arsenal. And you better upgrade from that Peter Gabriel song because it's been overdone. I spend every Saturday with a personal trainer who makes me throw up for fun, so I really don't want to hear about my pretty eyes or wit. Go ahead and bring it. Tell me I have a slamming body and get creative, dude, or I'm throwing you out and you won't get another chance to bang me."

God, she was magnificent. Beauty and brains. A slamming

body indeed along with a fine mind. Now, he couldn't get the *bang me* part out of his head as he hardened below again, ready to participate if Presley wanted to act out that part.

He'd call another woman out for playing games to gain his interest, but the best part? Presley Cabot couldn't care less if she impressed him or not. It was a total role reversal, and her brutal honesty was the biggest aphrodisiac he'd ever experienced.

"I think we both know your body is slamming, sweetheart. The kind to keep a man up at night, chanting your name when he comes in his fist, still unsatisfied because he didn't get to touch your skin or taste your lips. But you'd be much more than a release. You're the type of woman I want to linger with. Sink into. Dig deep. One I definitely would not want to let go, especially from my bed. There's much more underneath that body that's got me hard as a rock, and I intend to unearth every inch of her. How's that for bringing it?"

There. A flicker of wariness and raw emotion shone from her eyes, before being quickly masked. What was she hiding? Or was it just his massive ego thinking there was something more to her story than simple disinterest?

Didn't matter. There was no way he was letting this one slip away before figuring out why she stirred his gut and called to him on a deeper level he'd never experienced.

Oh, yeah.

He was going to bring it.

Presley called on every resource from the very fiber of her being to remain impassive.

She was failing on every level.

His words were pure heat sizzling between them, tiny pinpricks of fire that melted her insides and made her crave all the things he promised. All the things he wanted to do. All the things she'd let him do. If only she believed him. If only it wasn't more than this role she was playing, or her sexy dress, or her bare legs, or the perfect amount of cleavage. If only it was based on something more than their brief meeting and physical connection. But as much as she ached to believe him, she knew better. *Would Nolan even want the real Presley?*

He wouldn't be interested in the reality. The woman who wore thick reading glasses, dressed in flannel and cotton, and didn't own a thong. The woman who watched endless romcoms on classic DVDs and devoured a book every few days. The woman who was truly a loner, and only comfortable around her friends or family.

Nolan Banks was intrigued by a simple mirage she'd created to ensnare him.

It was critical she always remembered it.

Trinity had known immediately he'd try to finagle a surprise meeting, and when Presley saw the appointment on her calendar, she'd known it was him. The man was definitely impressive. He'd done enough research to know the name of the publisher she wanted to work with, and even managed to fool her receptionist—which was almost impossible to do. Too bad she was a few steps ahead of him due to her amazing revenge team. It was time to get back to the game.

She buried the pure female need pulsing in every cell and gave a snort. "Better," she said grudgingly. "But a bit cliché. I feel like I've read that line somewhere before. Plus, it's hard to believe when you've been staring at my cleavage like a man starving for air during your little speech."

"Actually, it was your legs," he said mildly. "And I think you wanted me to look my fill. It's part of the game, correct? And, Presley, I'm definitely starving . . . for *you*."

She snapped her gaze to him, afraid she'd given too much away, but those ocean blue eyes were filled with hot masculine appreciation and pure laughter. Teasing. Yes, he loved to tease. She used to eavesdrop on his conversations just to enjoy his sharp wit and generous humor. He had no problem making fun of himself, never taking anything too seriously. It was rare she'd met a man with a lack of arrogance but enough confidence to carry himself into the world. The combination made for a deadly attraction.

She quirked a brow. "A game that's coming to an end, Mr. Banks."

"How come you don't like me?" he challenged. "You came to meet me, remember?"

"I always introduce myself to the new members of our community. It's good business—not personal."

"Lie," he said softly. "I have a gut feeling this is deeply personal."

She pulled her gaze away, not trusting herself, and grabbed a stack of papers from her desk. "Then you're bound to be disappointed. Now, if there's nothing else you needed to discuss, my time is valuable. I need to deal with my real clients."

He ignored her dismissal and motioned to the pile of books teetering on the edge of her desk. "You publish Charlotte Sterling's work?"

She blinked in surprise. "Yes. Wait a minute—do you know her?"

"I know her work."

A bitter laugh escaped her lips. "Let me give you a head's up, beer man. Lying to try and score points will bring you nothing but my scorn and a kick out the door."

He cocked his head. Amusement and a touch of sympathy gleamed in those baby blues. "Bet you've been lied to a lot, huh? Probably by asshole men who thought they could manipulate you. By clients who thought a woman would be easy to railroad." He narrowed his gaze, ripping away the surface and diving into the murk she kept safely buried. "There's no way you can run a billion-dollar empire without getting your innocence shredded, constantly reminded that too many people are bound to disappoint. God knows, I've seen it firsthand. But I'm not one of those men, Presley. I don't lie. And I have no problem stating exactly what I want."

Her mouth dried up and an ache rose, spreading through her body like a virus. Dammit, why did he have to say stuff like that? Romantic. Poetic. Dominating. Charming. Like a romance book hero. Hell, she could keep falling for his ruse or he'd bury her alive. "As much as I admire your illusion of truth, I highly doubt you want to follow this one through. Let's just say you were mistaken and don't know Charlotte Sterling, shall we?"

"You don't believe me."

She gave an unladylike snort and tossed her head. "Hell, no. If you were going to try and impress me, you should've picked another writer."

As if scenting success, he leaned in with interest. "Wanna bet?"

Her gaze narrowed. "What do you mean?"

"I'll prove I'm not lying about Charlotte Sterling, and you have dinner with me."

"Thought you wanted to do lunch."

He gave a slow grin. "Now that the stakes are higher with your doubt of me, it's dinner."

Sparks shot between them. The air surged like an electrical current, and she caught her breath at the fierce sexual attraction between them. She shifted in her seat, and slowly eased her feet from her desk, breaking the stare. Her heart pounded so loud she was terrified he'd hear it. "What do I get when you lose?" she challenged.

"I leave you alone."

She tapped her nail on her lower lip. Tried to think. What was the best play? "Not a great win, beer man. How about something more substantial than your sparkling presence?"

He took the hit with a smile. "Name it, book goddess."

Her skin tingled from the nickname. The idea hit her full force. "You hold a romance novel event at your brewery showcasing LWW authors. This would include displaying their books and offering a special menu with beer pairings emphasizing romance."

"Oh, you're good. As blood-thirsty in business as pleasure. Just the way I like it."

"If you're done with the flattery, you can let me know if you accept the deal."

"Deal. Let's shake on it."

He stood up and offered his hand. She slowly copied his movement, trying to hide the slight hesitation. God, she was afraid to touch him, but it would be a good first test. If she succeeded with her plan, she'd not only need to touch him, but eventually kiss him. Butterflies took flight in her tummy, and she tipped her chin up in determination, closing her hand around his.

Fire. He was the fire burning every bit of her body.

Warm, strong fingers swallowed her hand in a firm grip, and his thumb stroked over the sensitive flesh of her wrist, registering her fluttering pulse. She couldn't help the tiny jerk and hitch of her breath as electricity sizzled between them. Desperately, she tried to tug her hand away, but he held on a few seconds longer, his gaze drilling into hers, forcing her to acknowledge the crazy chemistry bouncing off their linked hands.

For a few heart-stopping seconds, she fought the impulse to walk into his arms and let him hold her. To feel his body against hers one last time.

Instead, she finally managed to pull away and settled back into her chair. With the desk safely between them, she re-gathered her composure, morphing back to all-business mode. "Ready?" she asked. "I'll keep this simple."

"Go ahead."

"Name two of Charlotte Sterling's backlist books, and the current one out in bookstores right now."

He dragged in a breath and looked down at his hands. Satisfaction buzzed. There was no way he could do it. Charlotte was a well-known erotic romance writer, and her newest novel was pure women's fiction. Finally, he'd gambled on something he was about to lose. Minutes ticked by as the moment was drawn out. Finally, he looked up.

"*Crazy, Sexy, Sinful* is one of her backlist books. Another is *Yours, Mine, and Definitely Not Ours.* The series is called Wicked Boys After Dark and follows brothers with certain sexual penchants. Her brand-new book is called *Anything for Love*, but this one's not erotic. They're making a movie from it for the ME Time channel you own. Congrats to her on making the

USA Today list. Quite impressive in today's competitive market."

Her mouth fell open.

He rolled to his feet, stretching, and shot her a grin. "I'll pick you up at seven tonight."

He walked out of her office without a glance back.

Son-of-a-bitch.

She'd been played by the player.

CHAPTER 9

"Dude! Where you been? We've been waiting."

Nolan looked a bit annoyed as he stopped in front of a stocky guy with buzzed black hair, dark eyes, and muscles in all the right places. She didn't recognize him as one of his track buddies, but he looked vaguely familiar. "Had to put Carl to bed. What the hell did you make him drink, Gabe?"

Gabe laughed and took a swig of beer. "Just a few shots. He's got no tolerance. Who's this?"

She realized he was looking at her, his gaze traveling over her body in frank judgment. Presley stood to full height, desperately sucking in her stomach, and tried to look cool. "I'm Presley."

"Presley helped me with Carl," Nolan said. "I'm getting her a drink."

Gabe offered a grin, but he never looked into her eyes, only at her boobs. Her skin crawled with distaste. Nolan always kept eye contact. Was that a good or bad thing? "Hey, no need—got a new batch of my famous iced teas right here." He grabbed two red solo cups and a pitcher of tea, pouring a generous amount for both of them. "Here you go. Cheers!"

Nolan turned to her. "Want me to get you something else?" he asked.

Presley hesitated. She usually only drank beer or wine, and had sworn to her friends to never accept a drink she didn't pour herself. But she'd been watching Gabe pour the whole time, and didn't want to bring anymore attention to herself. She forced a smile. "No, this looks great. Cheers!" She tipped the rim to Nolan's and took a sip. The clash of hard liquor mixed with sweet tea burned her throat. She did her best not to choke. A few seconds later, a nice warm glow heated her blood. Hmm . . . she better watch herself with that stuff. It was potent.

"Good?" Gabe asked.

"Yes, thank you."

"Ready to really start this party?" he asked with a sly gleam in his dark eyes.

Nolan's jaw clenched. "I told you no to that shit, Gabe. I have a big meet this week."

Gabe snorted and waved his hand in the air. A touch of mean flicked his voice. "Sorry, I forgot you're better than your fraternity brothers."

"You don't have a scholarship you can screw up."

Gabe muttered something under his breath. "You're right. I'm not as smart as you. Or as fast. Or as rich. Better crawl back to the ghetto where I belong."

"Fuck. I didn't mean—"

Gabe walked away and got swallowed up by the crowd.

Sparks of frustration shot from his figure. Presley raised her voice over the sudden blast of music that screamed from the speakers. "Is he part of your fraternity?" she asked.

"Yeah."

"But not part of the track team?" she pressed.

Nolan shook his head. "Nah, he didn't make the team and I think he's still pissed. But as a fraternity brother, I try to get along with him. We're just different."

"We can't all get along with everyone," she pointed out. "Not everyone is going to like you."

His attention re-focused on her. "I hate when people don't like me. It's a problem."

She laughed with delight at his honesty. "Then this is good practice for you."

"I bet everyone likes you."

Shadows dimmed her humor for a few seconds. Her memory flashed on the endless images of people pointing and whispering behind her back, the cruel insults that flung her way when she walked into a room, and the disapproval of saleswomen when she tentatively asked if they carried a size 22. The world didn't like a fat person, and perhaps, that was one of the hardest things of all she dealt with regularly. But no way in hell was she revealing any of her darkest secrets.

Instead, she took another fortifying sip and fell back on her wit. "Because I don't care if people like me," she quipped. "It's the guaranteed way to make everyone fall over themselves for your approval. Pretend their opinions aren't important."

Suddenly, he leaned in. His warm breath struck her cheek. "Like you wrote about in your story?" he asked.

Presley froze. She didn't think he really listened when the Professor read other students' material. When she watched him from under heavily lidded eyes, he was always twitchy in his seat. Moving his long legs around, shifting his weight, closing his eyes as if stealing a cat nap. While up close, she spotted every graceful, sharp angle of his face. His eyes had a darker rim of navy at the outer edge, then a paler blue around the iris, adding to the intensity of his stare. His nose held *a slight tilt to the right. The scar on his brow was the shape of a Z. Maybe a rock? "You don't know what story I wrote."*

A smile touched his lips. "I remember now. You wrote about a girl attending her sixteenth birthday party. How she was surrounded by friends and family, but felt completely isolated, as if she was separated by a giant glass wall. Called it the insular effect. She could do anything she wanted behind the wall so it gave her a sense of freedom. But no connection."

The world shifted beneath her feet, but this time, it wasn't about his physical presence. No, this time, it was his words along with the intensity of his gaze and the connection surging between them. One of understanding and the acceptance of lies mixed with truth that showed up in their fiction. Her breath strangled in her lungs. "I can't believe you remembered that," she murmured.

"I can't believe I forgot. Or that I spent most of the semester not even knowing your name."

"Nolan! Get your ass over here for a minute—we need you!"

A roar of male voices reached her ears. He jerked away, a touch of annoyance on his face, then gave her a lopsided grin. "I better check out what they need."

Her tongue stuck to the roof of her mouth but she managed a nod. "Okay."

She watched his long-legged, hip rolling stroll across the room. The crowd of guys gave a cheer, opening up ranks, then closing around him. Her fingers gripped the solo cup. One mantra repeated itself over and over in her head.

Everything had changed.

She just had to decide what to do about it.

CHAPTER 10

"Honey bunch, I told you to stop squirming. Can't send you out to seduce a man with a crooked hem. Trinity would kill me."

Presley looked down at her friend, Cam Fong, who wielded a needle and thread like a weapon. He knelt at her feet, furiously fine-tuning the hem to his newest creation—a gorgeous black dress that practically floated over her body with grace and elegance. The moment Presley had called Trinity about her impromptu date, she'd sent over Cam to dress her for battle.

Cam was a graduate of Parson's Design and one of the best up-and-coming fashion designers. He'd been so damn talented that he'd scored a spot on Project Runaway, but gotten cut on the second round due to a horrific group challenge that turned into a plan to dump him early since he was a huge threat. Instead of fame and glory, and his own design studio, he took a job at a vintage clothing and costume shop in NYC, and focused on making the connections that would get him to be the next designer stylist to the stars. He had an eclectic, unique style that was slowly gaining attention, using his Chinese-American background along with his time spent in Hawaii. He used tons of bold, vibrant colors, paired with startling textures and angular design elements that added a wow factor.

Cam was Trinity's best friend and had been essential to transforming Presley from ugly duckling to swan after graduation, tucking her under his wing of protection and becoming fiercely devoted to her cause. He worked closely with Trinity to make sure all her outfits were perfection and created some of her own unique pieces. Presley had offered him numerous opportunities with LWW Enterprises, but he was stubborn and prideful, determined to do everything on his own steam. Instead, she wore his designs to her important functions and parties, telling everyone who'd listen about her amazing personal designer.

First, Presley had told her secretary to inform Nolan to meet her outside her office. It seemed safer and far less personal. Then she'd called Cam for advice, but he insisted on meeting her with his newest creation. Thank goodness she'd set up a private suite right off her office for assorted emergencies like cat naps, fashion crisis, or late-night meetings. The suite held a king size bed, a stocked bar, a full-sized dressing room bursting with clothes, accessories, and shoes, as well as a huge bathroom with walk in shower, and a make-up area with full lighting and mirrors in every size and angle.

"I'm sorry I made you come over tonight," she said. "I just didn't expect to be this freaked out."

He finished the hem and grabbed the steamer. "I've been dying to get you into this little black dress for a while, so it worked out fine. You need to arm yourself by connecting with your seductive, feminine power and show this monster a lesson." He shuddered in mock horror, his dark eyes gleaming with empathetic fury. His bright floral shirt and powder blue pants were immaculately stitched and fit his slim body perfectly. "You need to channel Phoebe Cates from *Lace*."

Presley laughed. Cam was obsessed with the old glamour and glitz television movies and books that used to be all the rage. She searched her memory. "Yeah, but she was trying to find her real mother, not wreak revenge on a man."

Cam waved a hand in the air. "It's super close and the fashion was amazing. That's what truly matters. Now, go look at yourself and tell me I'm pretty."

She stepped to the full-length beveled mirror and caught her breath.

The black dress was conservative in the front, the material covering her entire neck and stopping just below the chin. The fabric was sleek and light, so it moved effortlessly with her body, flaring slightly at the waist, and hitting just below the knee. But when she turned, that's when the magic happened.

Her back was entirely bare, as one strap of wide fabric tied around her neck in a collar, then spilled into three strings of luminescent pearls that fell to the top of her buttocks. It was outrageous and sexy but still classic.

Presley turned to her friend and blinked back tears. "You're so pretty, Cam. I love you so much."

"Aww, honey bunch, don't make me get all mushy. Make sure you're careful though, it's a delicate fabric and can rip easily. Now, do I need to go over the rules with you again?"

She groaned. "No, Aubrey already drilled me on the plan."

"Then fill me in so I can get my fine ass home."

"Be a little mean, but not enough to look like a bitch. Play hard to get, but then go all soft and seductive, like he's completely winning me over. Kiss him at the end of the night so he's begging for more. Leave him with a quip to keep him remembering me all night."

Cam sighed with pride. "My star. Now go get him."

"I will. Stay as long as you want." She gave her friend a hug, grabbed her Hermes bag, and strode out the door in her black Manolos. Cam loved her private suite and would probably uncork some champagne and watch Netflix on her comfy bed. He always said it was a thrill to know a stuffy corporate environment lay right outside the door.

She smiled and greeted each employee by name as she made her way downstairs, and walked out of the lobby.

Before she even spotted him, as if she had a six sense, she knew he was waiting for her.

Her body slammed into high alert, softening in all her girly places and hardening her nipples beneath the delicate silk that didn't offer the safety of a bra. He stood on the sidewalk, hands in his pockets, looking calm, cool, and collected. He gave off the lazy languor of a resting panther, yet held an edge of sharpness that told her he'd been patiently waiting for her arrival. Her gaze ate him up with a gnawing hunger that betrayed her, pissing her off. This man was, at heart, a jerk. Yet, Presley knew if he touched her, she'd turn into a bunch of silly putty with no spine and no pride.

Damn him.

He looked devastatingly hot. All those hard, lean muscles were contained in black slacks, a Robert Graham button down pink shirt with overlarge cuffs, and a black fitted casual jacket. Those oaky curls were thick and just a bit mussed to keep him from looking pretty.

But it was his eyes that always got her, holding her captivate as they possessed her. Bluer than the Caribbean Sea, with a mix of mischief and hot sex. Friend and lover. Jock and bad boy. Charmer and seducer. The ultimate combination of kryptonite to women.

Including her.

He walked over to meet her, his stare taking in her outfit with male appreciation. "You look gorgeous," he said, truth ringing in his voice. "Thank you for accepting my date."

She lifted a brow, keeping her voice cool. "I lost the bet, remember?"

He shot her a grin, offering his arm as an escort. "Let's forget about the circumstances that brought you here. I promise to dazzle you so much tonight, you'll forget you were forced in my company."

She couldn't help her smile. He was just too affable about the insult. She took his arm. "Fine. Where are we going?"

"Dinner. It's about half an hour with traffic. I'd like to surprise you."

She studied him under her lashes. "Ah, I love a good mystery. I'm in your capable hands."

His hand stiffened on her arm at her low, throaty growl. But the joke was on her when a wash of heat poured into her veins and her breath caught. She had to be careful when playing such a dangerous game. God knows, she didn't want to fall into her own trap.

He escorted her to a sleek black BMW, opened the door, and guided her into the seat.

She knew the moment he caught sight of the back of her dress.

The air tightened with sensual tension, and he eased her

close to his chest, his breath a hiss against her ear. *"Fuck."* The softly muttered curse spilled from his lips. Instead of ignoring him, she waved the red cloth in front of the bull, tilting her head up to meet his gaze head on. "Is there a problem?" she drawled.

She expected a touch of frustration. Instead, he shook his head in admiration, his heated gaze raking over the naked skin exposed. "You really are a magnificent creature," he murmured, his breath a soft rush of warmth against her cheek. He smelled of sandy beaches and fresh washed cotton. Presley had a crazy impulse to lay her head against his chest and breathe in his unique scent, remembering in a flash lying naked in his arms, those few precious seconds of heady joy and intimacy after sex. He stared at her for a few seconds, stretching out the delicious tension, but she managed to grab her composure, turning away and taking her seat.

She had one mission to fulfill. After that, she'd keep her distance from Nolan Banks and lock him back into her past.

He began driving, heading out of Port Hudson. He was a relaxed driver, his grip easy over the wheel, and adept at weaving through the heavy traffic without sudden stops and starts. She decided to begin taking charge of the conversation, curious as to what had happened to him over the years. She crossed her legs and eased back into the seat. "So, Nolan Banks. Tell me all your secrets."

"Oh, hell no. Not until I've plied you with expensive Rosé first. I have to keep you intrigued, at least to dessert."

His grin was contagious. She remembered how he'd flash it after winning a big race, inviting a roar of support and admiration from his teammates, even though he also competed against them. "At least, tell me why you wanted to open up a bar in the same town as your brother?"

He winced. "Ah, you know about Carter?"

"Quarters has been around a while and has a loyal clientele. Are you enemies or something?"

"Frenemies," he corrected. "I love my brother but we've always had this rivalry going on since we were young."

"Was he a Wall Street guy like you and your parents?" she asked.

"Yes. Carter, me, and Landon, my sister, were all groomed to work at Banks Finance. Unfortunately, my brother and I never wanted anything to do with that life. After I graduated from college, I talked about opening up a craft beer bar in town, but I'd agreed to try working in the family business for a minimum of two years if they paid for college. It was a fair deal and I had to stick it out."

"Did Carter make the same compromise?"

Nolan nodded. "Of course. He's three years older than me, so the bastard did his time, then announced he was moving to Port Hudson to open a pub."

"You must've been pissed."

"Let's just say we got into a bit of a tussle, but there was nothing I could do. He even stole the name I'd planned to use, though he swears it was his idea first."

She laughed. "I'd say The Bank tops Quarters. He must've been quite surprised when you showed up in town building a new microbrewery."

He grinned. "Hell, yes. It was worth everything to see the look on his face when he saw the flyer pinned to the door of his pub. He went apeshit—it was awesome."

She shook her head. "I don't understand men. Women would never forgive one another."

"Trust me, I'd never do something like that to Landon. First off, she's tougher than both of us and would seriously kick my ass."

"I think I'd like her."

"I know you would. You have any siblings?"

"No, just me. But I'm close with my parents."

"Tell me how you started LWW Enterprises. What's the story behind it?"

Unease slithered within. How much did he really know about her? And if he'd Googled her like she expected, wouldn't he make the connection between her graduating from Boyer University? God, she figured that would have sparked some type of memory for him! But if he did know, why would he be going through this entire charade, pretending not to know who she was? She chewed on the inside of her cheek and considered her options.

"Presley? You didn't fund the company on dirty money or gambling, did you?"

She swiveled her gaze to his. "How much do you know about me?" she asked.

"Not much."

More lies? Was he playing a bigger, smarter game than she imagined? Did he really not have a clue who she was at this point? "How about laying our cards on the table, Nolan?" she challenged. "I bet the moment you figured out my full name, you researched every detail on the Net. Armed yourself with a bunch of information in order to play me the right way. If you did, you'll realize one big thing. I can take anything but a liar."

He jerked, but she didn't back down. If her whole plan was

going down in smoke, she might as well play the entire scenario out. She may not get her full revenge, but at least she'd force him to confront his nasty actions and take some responsibility. Anger whipped up inside as she waited for the big confrontation.

He eased into the right lane, heading north on the Thruway. "Presley, I'm sorry if I pissed you off, but I swear I'm telling the truth. I called Carter and asked who you were. He told me about LWW Enterprises and that you'd lived in the town for a number of years, and that you were single. That's it. I'm not going to Google a woman I'm interested in and try to learn crap from social media or other news sources that may not give me the full picture. I want you to tell me who you are. I want us to get to know one another on our own terms. And as for lying? Don't want to disappoint you, sweetheart, but like I stated before, I don't lie. Much easier to take the punishment of the moment telling the truth, then the slow torture that a lie can do."

His words cut through her, attacking like a dozen paper cuts. Dear Lord, he sounded so sincere. Her stupid heart had actually squeezed in longing at the beauty of those words, at believing he really was the type of man she could trust and be with in a romantic way.

But he was a proven liar. Maybe he hadn't Googled her, but inside, he was still untrustworthy. Still, the plan was all set and there was no reason to back off now, especially since he still had no clue he'd once slept with her as a cruel joke.

Fine.

Game on.

She made herself reach out and touch him, squeezing his arm in reassurance. "I'm sorry, Nolan. I believe you. It's just that

in my position, I've had many men who pursued me with some-
what dishonorable intentions."

The sugar worked well. He cut her a sympathetic glance and
nodded. "I get it. Hell, I can only imagine how hard it is for you
to be a big fish in a little pond. Let's just take the night and see
where it leads. Deal?"

"Deal."

On cue, one of her favorite songs, *Meant to Be* by Florida
Georgia Line came over the radio, and they both shared a
glance and began laughing. "Let's table my questions 'til dinner.
We're here."

He took the exit for Suffern and followed the winding
roadway that twisted higher up the mountain. The low squat-
ting building surrounded by gardens seemed as if it was
dropped straight from Japan, luring customers into another
culture. Mount Fuji was known for their exquisite setting and
food, and was one of Presley's favorite restaurants.

Nolan parked the car. "I hope you like Japanese food," he
said, his face reflecting a flicker of worry.

"I adore it," she said. "It's a perfect choice."

Her insides shouldn't have sighed with pleasure at his
pleased grin, or the way he opened her door and escorted her
inside with a hand under her elbow. They were brought to their
table in the private gardens, where vibrant-colored, fat pillows
lined the low wooden table, beautifully set with candles and an
array of ceramic plates and bowls. Bamboo screens shrouded
them in a world of their own.

Presley sank to the floor and settled on a ruby cushion,
wiping her hands with the hot towels served by prongs. The
server bowed and greeted them. She wore a red kimono robe,
and her black hair was caught up in an elaborate bun.

Nolan leaned over. "Would you mind if I ordered for both of us?" Usually, Presley disliked heavy handed mannerisms, but he seemed to genuinely want to please her, so this time, she nodded. "Is there anything you're allergic to or don't prefer? Do you eat sushi?"

"No, I'm fine with anything and I love sushi."

"Wonderful."

Nolan lifted his head to meet the server's gaze and began speaking in Japanese.

Presley watched in pure shock. The sexy sound of his voice talking so elegantly in another language hit her straight in the solar plexus. Fascinated, she watched the server light up, and engage animatedly with him as she scribbled down his selections on the pad, then disappeared.

"I figured we'd start with some hot sake, then switch to Rosé but let me know if you feel like something else."

"You speak Japanese?"

Was that a touch of red blooming on his cheeks? That cleft in his chin deepened every time he smiled, and she was beginning to obsess over it as much as the scar. "Yes, I needed to learn the language if I wanted to do my job on Wall Street. We work with international clientele on a global market, so I made sure I was fluent in four languages."

She blinked. "Four? What are they?"

He ticked them off his fingers. "Spanish, Japanese, Chinese, and German."

"Holy crap! That's really good."

"I would've told you that earlier if I'd known it'd impress you," he teased.

"I'm much more impressed by brain power than biceps," she said, taking a sip of water. "Most can't even master the English language. You should see some of the horrific writing that passes my desk. It's a sin."

"I can imagine. I was lucky. Languages always came easy to me."

"Everything came easy to you," she said, settling her napkin on her lap.

"What do you mean?" he asked with a frown. "How would you know that?"

Shit. She revealed too much. His essay was still imprinted on her brain—the way he described how it felt being good at everything he tried. Instead of being arrogant, his words revealed a stark honesty and raw unveiling of doubt. But he didn't remember they sat in writing class together or shared their work.

The arrival of their drinks and appetizers was the perfect distraction, and by the time she'd bitten into a crispy spring roll, he'd forgotten his question.

She'd have to be more careful.

CHAPTER 11

HE HADN'T COME BACK.

Presley's high spirits had dimmed. Nolan hadn't sought her out again, choosing to stay with his friends. She'd caught sight of him about half an hour ago, but now he'd disappeared.

She went to the kitchen to dump her cup, gather her friends, and leave. Still, she had to count the evening as a success. Maybe he'd talk to her in class now. Maybe she'd ramp up her courage and ask him to coffee. She didn't know if it was worse her dreams of him were as good as reality because now her obsessive crush had turned even more intense.

Smothering a sigh, she found the trash and threw away the rest of her drink. The world tilted slightly and her focus was touched with mist. Yeah, she was definitely tipsy, and on her way to more. Next time, she'd stick to wine. Those homemade cocktails were deadly.

"Been looking for you, babe."

She looked up as Gabe loomed over her, a big grin on his face. She stepped back for more space. "What's up?"

"Nolan's looking for you. Said he wanted to see you. Alone."

His emphasis on the last word curled with a smirk. She blinked, narrowing her gaze, but that damn mist had taken hold again. "Nolan wants to see me alone?" she repeated.

"Yep. He's been asking for you. Hey, you're dry. Need another drink?"

She shook her head. "No, thank you. Where is he?"

Gabe jerked his chin. "Back bedroom, right side."

She frowned, her Spidey senses tingling. "He's alone in there?"

"Yeah, I told you. He's waiting for you." He gave a creepy wink. "Have fun."

Gabe walked away. She hesitated, not sure if she should just walk into an empty bedroom. She'd seen all those Lifetime movies about date rape. It was an important reason her friends watched who poured their drinks and that they always checked up on one another. First, she'd tell Aubrey and Libby where she was heading, and ask them to wait for her. If things went well between her and Nolan, and Gabe wasn't lying, she could tell them to safely leave.

After assuring her friends, she headed down the hall, and opened the door to the bedroom. Her nerves tingled with anticipation.

"Nolan?" she called out.

The room was simple, yet cluttered. Clothes strewn around, a beat-up mustard chair in the corner covered with papers, and a low coffee table held an array of cups, soda bottles, and chips. Immediately, her focus went to the bed. She had a crappy, twin mattress in her dorm that sounded like crackers when she moved. This one was king sized and dwarfed the room. Nolan was spread out on top of the white sheets, arms tucked under his head, his back toward her. His weight shifted and a low moan filled the air. Was he okay? Was he sick?

She hurried into the room and leaned over him. Steady puffs of breath released from his full lips, and his brow was smooth and relaxed. Waves of toasty brown hair fell over his closed eyes.

He was asleep.

Disappointment crashed over her. She stared into his perfect face, the need and longing rising up inside to touch him, kiss him, bury her face against his shoulder and breathe in his scent. Biting her lip, she tentatively brushed the strands of hair from his brow, admiring the dark, thick lashes and golden tint to his skin.

Slowly, she pulled her hand away.

In one sudden movement, his eyes flew open and his fingers grasped her wrist.

Presley gasped. His gaze locked with hers. She tumbled into a vast ocean of blue. The heat of his skin burned, his grip tightening as they stared at one another for endless, heart-stopping moments.

Then with a groan, he yanked her toward him and kissed her.

The shock of his lips over hers kept her frozen in place, caught between fantasy and reality. He didn't seem to care about her stillness. His kiss was a tempting seduction, not an arrogant claiming. As if sensing she was hesitant, his mouth moved slowly over hers, his tongue tracing the tight seam of her lips, sipping at the hint of her essence as if asking permission to enter.

The entire world stilled, tilted, and hung over the abyss.

Her heart stuttered, her body clenched, and her eyes shut as she opened her lips.

His tongue surged inside to play, drinking her in, his hands moving up to cup her cheeks and hold her still. He kissed her like a drowning man who needed air. He kissed her like the last woman on earth. He kissed her like she was everything he ever craved and everything he ever needed.

Presley let out a cry, leaning toward him, her hands frantically burying into the crisp, sleek strands of his hair. She fell completely into him, letting him take and pleasure, and realized that he had ruined her for kissing any other man for the rest of her life.

"Taste so good," he groaned, nipping at her lips, taking the kiss even deeper. "Want more."

"Yes," she breathed out, her needy body practically weeping for everything he could give her. "I just have to tell my friends. I'll be right back."

"Don't go." He kissed her jaw, stroking her hair, as he pulled her down on top of him.

"I promise I'll be right back. Don't move."

With a herculean effort of Wonder Woman, she disentangled herself and stumbled toward the door. The sights and sounds of the party slammed into her, wrenching her from the dreamlike quality he'd woven when he kissed her. Desperate to return, she hurriedly pushed her way into the living room where Aubrey and Libby waited.

"You guys can go now," she said, her tongue tripping over the flurry of words. "I'm staying with Nolan tonight."

Aubrey gasped. "No fucking way! I knew you could do it—he'd be nuts not to fall for you. Babe, I'm so happy. Do you have condoms?"

She shook her head. "No."

"Remember the rules? No condoms, no sex. Here, I have a few in my stash." She rummaged through her bag, proudly taking out a handful and pressed them into her palm. "One is super-sized so let's hope you can use it."

Libby giggled. "Got a vibrator in there, too?"

"Actually, I do. You never know when you need to liven up a string of boring classes."

Presley choked with laughter. "Thanks, guys. Love you."

"Are you sure you're going to be okay here?" Libby asked with a frown. "I don't like fraternities. Maybe I'll stay here and crash on the couch."

"I'm fine—I'm in Nolan's room and we're alone."

"Okay, take care of you," Libby said.

"Take care of you," she repeated back. Ever since they watched Pretty Woman that night, they'd all adopted the caretaking phrase for each other.

Hiding the condoms in her fist, Presley headed back to the room where Nolan was waiting for her.

CHAPTER 12

Nolan watched her bite into the spring roll and wondered again what he seemed to be missing.

Her comment brought a rumbling of distant memories, but none of them were clear enough to grab onto. It had been something about himself he'd always carried like a dark secret. Silly, yes. While other people struggled, he seemed to move forward like the path before him was paved in grease. From sport trophies to grades to Wall Street, he never had to struggle. He worried he'd take his life for granted, so he worked even harder to appreciate every small detail and gift bestowed on him, burying his guilt and trying to never complain, even when he felt trapped in the success of his own making.

Opening the brewery was the first time he'd been scared to fail. The first time success suddenly had a deeper meaning, and the hunger from within finally clawed to the surface.

Every time he looked at Presley, he felt that same hunger. It was as if he sensed in his soul she was the woman who could finally satisfy him, on every level. There was a familiarity about her that he couldn't place, something even more powerful than the chemistry that surged between them, something that screamed *serendipity.*

Of course, if he told her all that she'd run screaming for the exit. Way too much and too soon. He'd have to ease her into the idea by charming the pants off her.

Figuratively, and hopefully, literally.

"It's time to spill. How do you know Charlotte Sterling?" she demanded, taking a sip of her wine.

He tapped a chopstick on the edge of his plate. "If I tell you, I'll need your promise not to blackmail me."

"Sorry, I can't promise. Now man up and confess."

She truly was ruthless. Why did he find her so appealing? "Fine, your sweet words convinced me. I happen to enjoy reading romance."

She blinked and stared hard at him. A little frown furrowed her brow. "For the sex?"

He chuckled. "The sex is an added bonus, but no, it's not the real reason. I read everything I can get my hands on. My sister actually gave me a book by Marina Adair after I was acting like an asshole, and told me to start reading romance to understand women better. I read it, bought another one, and began reading more in the genre. I picked up Charlotte Sterling and got hooked."

"For the sex?"

He couldn't help but play a bit. He leaned over the table, gaze pinning her in place. "Hmm, I'm surprised. For a smart, savvy publisher, you push sex in your clients' books a lot. I mean, sex sells to a certain degree. But romance is really about the emotion, you know."

Her cheeks got all flush and pink. She sputtered in outrage. "I know that! There's just not tons of men reading it for the prose. I have every right to be suspicious."

He crossed his arms and began to recite. *"The moonlight trickled through the window, illuminating the rough edges of his face, emphasizing the almost ugly play of bone and muscle that made up the features of the man she'd begun to fall in love with during the night. Those few precious hours where her soul had not just been seen for the very first time, but recognized, embraced, and cherished."*

The quote fell in the air between them and lingered in resulting silence.

This time, he was the one who fought a blush. Dammit, it'd been too much. She was going to think he was not only a player, but a true nerd, and dump his ass right here and now.

Instead, those gorgeous smoky eyes widened and softened. A smile played about her lips, and for the first time since they'd met, she seemed completely open to him. He gazed deep, humbled at the opportunity to *see* her, his head spinning from the misty longing in her face as she stared at him.

"That was beautiful," she whispered. "I can't believe you remembered that section in Charlotte's work. It wasn't even part of the sex scene."

"I remembered the sex stuff, too. Her heroes are very good with rope."

Another laugh. "My favorite part about her writing is how she can grab this moment and wring out all the feelings from a reader. I think we forget to stop and experience the totality of what we're given, you know? I don't want to waste my time. I want to pause and revel in the physical and emotional pieces of my moments, even if they're jagged and sometimes painful." She paused, as if picking through her thoughts to better describe herself. He held his breath, studying the flickering expressions on her beautiful face. "Books make it easy to feel and be vulnerable. That's probably why I love reading so much."

"Me, too. Books are also safer."

"Yeah. Sometimes, I wish I was braver. To push more outside of the pages."

Was that a trace of sadness in her voice or his imagination? He reached across the table and snagged her fingers, needing the contact. "Somehow, I think you're one of the bravest women I've ever met."

Startled, her gaze met his and connected. Her fingers squeezed around his, causing a warmth to spread across his body. And in that one perfect moment, Nolan felt things he'd never felt before.

The server glided in to check on them, bowing politely before quietly exiting.

Presley pulled her hand back. He already mourned the warmth of her touch, the slight sting of her nails against his palm. But he allowed her the space, reminding himself he'd already pushed too hard. "So, how did LWW Enterprises get started?" he asked, keeping the dialogue neutral.

"I always dreamed of running my own business in publications and editing—I knew it was a gift I had. I could look at a book and know exactly how to fix it to make the story stronger. One night, I got drunk with my best friends, Aubrey and Libby, and we conceived this business based on Ladies Who Write. We wanted a company that could grow, with different media arms led by each of us. It took us a while to develop a working business plan and get the funding."

"I'm surprised you were able to secure such a large loan without collateral," he said.

"Well, we got a bit of a head start. My grandfather was quite wealthy, and since I was his only granddaughter, when he passed, he willed me a large chunk of money with one disclaimer."

He cocked his head. "What?"

She lifted her sake in a mock toast. "Use it to do something I believed in. He stressed it should be reckless and a pure passion project. The initial deposit helped secure all the loans we needed, and all three of us are now full partners. Together, we were able to expand globally and make a real difference in this world."

His smile was full of pride. "You are one amazing woman."

She tipped back her cup and drained her sake. "Yeah, but I only speak English."

He laughed, enjoying the look of pleasure on her face. He felt as if he was slowly chiseling away her guarded exterior, and he loved every second. But it was only moments later, a cloud passed over her face, and she suddenly withdrew into herself. Almost as if she was reminding herself to keep her distance. A trickle of disappointment leaked through him.

"Where did you go?" he asked softly.

Her eyes widened. Why did she look so torn? As if letting herself relax around him was a crime? Why was she fighting their attraction so hard? She gripped her chopsticks in a death hold, as if trying to come to terms with a decision.

"Presley?"

The spell seemed to break, and right before his eyes, she began to change. She gave him a slow smile, stretching her shoulders back, which thrust her breasts forward like a gift that begged to be unwrapped and treasured. On cue, his gaze dropped and his body roared to life, imagining the weight of her breasts through the thin silk, the way his fingers would play with and pleasure her nipples. How she'd tremble in his arms and whisper her name, arching and aching for more.

He shifted on the pillow, trying to conceal his hardness below. Holy shit, he had to get himself under control. He was like a teenager around her, thinking only with his little head.

Or in this moment, the big one.

She upped the stakes and casually reached out to stroke his fingers, raking her nails over the back of his hand in a teasing gesture. Goosebumps peppered his arm from the gesture. "So, what's your preferred poison?" she drawled, her voice a curl of smoke, teasing and seductive in his ears.

He blinked as if in a fog. What was the question? "Huh?"

She gave a throaty laugh. "Work-out. You don't drink beer for a living and look like this without working for it."

He didn't even remember how this subject had come up, but he had no brain cells to try and figure it out. Nolan had to think hard to remember what he did. "Oh. Right. I like to run."

She ran her tongue over her bottom lip, as if considering his answer. He pinned his hungry gaze to her mouth. "How fascinating. I've heard running does all sorts of good things for the body. Builds muscles." She squeezed his hand, then stroked up his arm. The fabric of his sports coat denied him the full experience of her hand on his skin but his biceps still flexed in response. "Power." She leaned all the way forward to close the distance, the tips of her breasts barely brushing his chest. "And the most important of all."

She waited. His head spun. Was that a tiny groan that escaped his lips? She was tying him up in knots. His voice came out ragged. "What's that?"

Presley tossed her hair and pursed her lips, inches from his.

Her whispered words promised a trip to both heaven and hell, so pleasurable he'd take both. "Endurance. You do have *endurance*, don't you, Nolan?"

His breath came out in a pant, and he stared at her helplessly. Pure triumph gleamed in her smoky eyes. It took him a few moments to battle through the erotic trance she'd spun on him, but he slowly realized she wanted him like this. Hard. Wanting. Confused.

The question he couldn't figure out was *why*. Why was she teasing him when it seemed obvious that she wasn't going to let herself have more? It was as if he was with two different personalities, twisted into one intriguing, maddening female. She began to ease back, as if satisfied with her win.

Oh, no. He wasn't letting her off the hook that easy.

His hand shot out and grasped her upper arm. She jerked back, her eyes wide with surprise. He kept his voice low and easy. "There's one other activity I like. Helps a lot with all the things you listed."

Her brow arched. She somehow spoke without a hitch in her breath, but he could practically feel her arousal soaking the air. "Oh, really? What's that?"

He grinned slowly. Tilting his head, he pulled her to him in one easy movement. His gaze drilled into hers, and he spotted a raw hunger there she couldn't hide. "Sex."

He waited for her smart answer, but she remained silent. Amusement cut through him, and he pushed his advantage, wanting her flustered in his arms. Wanting her off balance around him. "What do you think about sex, Presley?"

She licked her lips, but this time, it didn't look practiced. She looked nervous. "Sex is . . . good."

His body roared like a primitive caveman, craving to mark

her with is scent. His touch. His mouth. Knowing any moment she could recover and change back into the role of savvy, challenging seductress, he moved with lightning speed. Cupping her cheeks, his lips hovered an inch away. His warm breath struck her mouth. "Sweetheart, if that's the only adjective that comes to mind, you're not getting the right exercise."

She softened in his arms. Her lips parted. Her eyes half closed, and she tilted her head up, ready to kiss him back.

With every last ounce of willpower, Nolan remained still and memorized the graceful features of her face, the beauty of her surrender that he swore he'd gain again, on his terms.

He lowered his head the last few inches.

His mouth brushed hers like a whisper.

Then, he drew back.

Her eyes flew open.

Ignoring his body's grumpy demands to take what was offered, he gave her a smile. "I intend to change that." His declaration was a total masculine challenge, but instead of a smart comeback, she just stared at him. His heart squeezed in his chest. "But first, let's eat."

The server re-appeared with a full staff carrying endless platters. He allowed her the space and time to settle back in, noticing she seemed to focus all her attention on her meal.

Sushi and sashimi of tuna, salmon, and eel were displayed beautifully amidst steaming plates of noodles, fresh vegetables, teriyaki chicken, filet mignon, and seaweed salad. "This could feed a small country," she said, plucking a rainbow tuna roll and dipping it into the wasabi soy sauce. "How did you know I like to eat?"

"I didn't," he said. He wondered about the sharp edge to her voice. "I wanted to learn what food was your favorite, what you disliked, and what made you smile when the flavors hit your tongue. A woman enjoying her food is like a holy experience. Kind of like sex."

"I hate to break it to you, beer man, but I've enjoyed both and still haven't forgotten the peppercorn encrusted filet at Peter Luger's. The experience lasted longer and was a hell of a lot more fulfilling."

He grinned, enjoying her smart wit. "Fascinating. It's usually the chocolate truffles or carbs that takes a man down."

She shrugged. "Pasta and pizza are great foreplay. The chocolate is the satisfying epilogue."

"Ah, there's my answer." He reached over and took a chunk of meat from the platter, then brought it to her lips. "Open for me, Presley," he murmured.

She obeyed, parting her lips and allowing him to place the chunk of filet on her tongue. He watched her chew, her face adorned in pleasure, and barely tamped down a primal growl of need. "You're a carnivore at heart," he said, reaching out to dab at her mouth with a napkin. His eyes burned with emotion. "And you just issued a challenge I won't be able to resist."

She rolled her eyes and took a sip of her wine. "Let me guess. As a big, strong, virile man you shall show me the greatest sex of my life, provide multiple orgasms, and wipe out all memories of any other men until I admit being in bed with you is better than any steak I ever had."

His lips quirked at her droll tone. "I was thinking more in the lines of providing you with the perfect meal to wipe out the memory of Luger and replace it with what I can give you." He reached over and tucked a wayward strand of hair behind her ear, then traced the line of her jaw with his index finger, eliciting a tiny shudder. "But I like your challenge better, one where you'd be screaming my name from those luscious lips, begging me to never stop."

She looked so startled, he couldn't help laughing. He lifted her hand and pressed a kiss to her palm. "I'm sorry, sweetheart, I couldn't resist. Now, let me prove I have more to offer than some decent quips and sexual innuendoes. I want to know why you chose to edit romance as your main genre."

She relaxed and bit into a crunchy piece of broccoli. "Romance gives you hope," she said simply. "I'm consistently thrilled and challenged by the spectrum of stories in the genre. Helping shape a writer's vision into a story that readers love is the truest form of work I can ever do in this life."

Her answer entranced him. She was a true romantic and gentle at heart. "That's one of the most beautiful things I've ever heard. It was never about the money or power, was it?"

"Money and power is nice," she said slowly. "I can't lie. You have more freedom and opportunities and I never take that for granted. But at the end of the day, I want to sleep at night, and knowing my work was meaningful is the most important thing to me."

"Yes, that's why I left Wall Street. There was no inner fulfillment. I felt hollow inside. Like I was living someone else's life, even though I had money, connections, and was at the top of the power chain. Everyone wanted to be me except . . . me."

"Why beer?"

He laughed. "It's my way of being creative. There's something about mixing the right blend of flavors and hops to make something completely unique. I love watching a group of friends gather at a place they love, to shoot the shit and enjoy a few beers. It's part of a memory of family, friends, and good times." He gave her a sheepish look and shrugged. "Probably sounds stupid and juvenile, I know, but it's just the way I see it."

"I get it."

Her words held truth. Somehow, he believed she did, and that only made him more determined to pursue her. He smiled and she returned his smile with one of her own, causing a rush of warmth that flushed through him. Their connection crackled and sizzled like a live wire, and he was hopeful for the rest of the evening ahead.

CHAPTER 13

THE FIRST THING SHE DID WAS TURN OFF THE LIGHTS.

She'd whispered his name a few times, but was greeted with only silence, and the soft whoosh of his breathing. But she didn't hesitate. She'd been crushing on him for too long to let this opportunity pass. Nolan Banks wanted her. He was the man she'd give her virginity to.

Shivering slightly, she stopped beside the bed and undressed. Getting the extra tight Spanx over her hips was difficult. Thank God he was asleep because she'd never be able to perform a sexy striptease with those on. Dropping the condoms on the side table, she slid into bed next to him, naked, closing her eyes and waiting for him to wake up and reach for her.

Nothing happened.

Frustrated, she turned her head to gaze at him. Okay, she'd have to wake him up again. Gently. God knows, she'd lose her nerve if she stayed too long in his bed with no clothes on and nothing happening. She reached out tentatively and touched his shoulder. Hard muscle shifted under soft cotton and made her fingertips tingle. He murmured something under his breath, rolled over, and threw his arm across her chest.

Oh. My. God.

She began to shake, the tingling spreading from her fingers to each part of her body. Liquid warmth flowed through her veins. If she felt this good before anything happened, how amazing would the sex be?

Reaching deep for courage, she moved her hand from his shoulder to his rough cheek, down to his jaw, enjoying the slight scratch of stubble. "Nolan?" she whispered, leaning closer. "Are you awake?"

The hand tightened, then moved upward. A slight frown creased his brow, and then he was tugging the sheet away impatiently, finally hitting her bare breast. Her heart stopped, then skittered madly in an uneven rhythm as his palm cupped her, his thumb sliding over her hardening nipple.

She didn't move. Didn't breathe. Just savored the delicious sensation of his talented fingers and the melting in the pit of her stomach.

"Feels so good," he slurred. His hand squeezed gently, ripping a groan from her lips, and suddenly he was on top of her, his mouth taking over where his fingers had been. She gasped in shock as his hot, wet tongue flicked over her nipple, shooting sparks to her pussy, which grew damp and achy. Her arms came up and she buried her fingers in his hair, holding his head close, lost in the wicked sensation of his mouth on her intimate parts that had never even seen a man's gaze, let alone his touch. He moved to her other breast, and his hard erection pressed against her inner thigh, still blocked by the sheet. Thrilled that she was turning him on, she gripped his hair tighter, and spread her legs, wanting some pressure to ease the empty ache inside. He nipped at her bottom lip and roughly tore the rest of the sheet off, leaving her naked, but she was too far gone to be embarrassed at her weight now, caught up in her fantasy finally coming to life.

He tugged at the zipper of his jeans, managing to wriggle them over his hips, then yanked down his underwear. She couldn't see in the dark, but he felt pretty big against her inner thigh. Presley slid her hand from his hair and down the muscled length of his chest, down toward his dick, and finally, grasped it in her hands.

Oh, yes.

A curse blistered his lips as she stroked him, and a sense of heady power whipped through her. He was huge, thick, and hot. She'd never touched a guy's cock before, but she finally realized why it was so amazing. He grew bigger in her grasp, and so she squeezed gently and his hips thrust toward her, as if he was caught in the grip of a fever.

"God, yes. So good."

And then he was touching her between her legs, his fingers rubbing her clit just enough to make her squirm for more, parting her thighs with hard hands, rearing up and pressing his dick toward—

"Condom," she gasped, pulling back frantically.

He stared at her in a fog, blinking, paused at her entrance. Reaching over to the table, she grabbed one, ripping open the wrapper and handing him the condom. He shook his head as if to clear it. "Sorry, sorry," he grunted, his fingers stumbling with the rubber, rolling it over his erection.

The interruption had made her nervous again, so she hoped he'd stroke her gently between her legs again to give her that awesome feeling, but foreplay must've been done because he immediately pushed inside her with one long, hard thrust.

Ah, shit.

It hurt. She winced as all pleasure faded, and her body wept from the invasion. She wriggled underneath him, trying to get past the discomfort, but then his mouth was over hers and he was kissing her in that deep, soft, sexy way he'd done before, and some of the tenseness left her body and she began to relax.

His hands rubbed her nipples and he began pushing in and out of her. A tightening began in her lower body, and she reveled in the hot thrust of his tongue along with his talented fingers, and the way his dick buried deeply inside her. She began to loosen up and crave more, meeting his thrusts with a demand of her own.

He ripped his mouth from hers and threw his head back. She gazed at his beautiful face, all tight and focused, his lips slightly parted. Suddenly he was shouting, his hips jerking madly as he came, and she reveled in every moment of his orgasm and the feminine power that gripped her.

With a satisfied groan, he pulled out of her and rolled over. He flung one arm over her, holding her close, and without another word, collapsed back into the pillow.

Then remained silent.

Presley waited for a bit, positive he was just re-gaining his strength, but then his soft snores cut through the silence.

He'd gone back to sleep.

She lay beside him, her thighs sticky, her skin damp with sweat, and felt a flicker of disappointment.

That was it?

Frustration nipped at her. It certainly hadn't been spectacular, like she'd fantasized. And it hurt much more than she expected. But the kissing was awesome. She'd also enjoyed the way he responded to her, and maybe if he'd lasted longer she could have gotten closer to that elusive orgasm. But it was their first time, and they needed to get to know one another. Presley was positive it would be better the next time.

She figured she'd use the bathroom and tried to ease away from him, but he muttered a long string of words and hugged her tighter, cuddling her into his chest. Her heart melted and her body sighed with pleasure. This was the best part. Being held in his arms like she was treasured was worth it all.

Presley relaxed, closed her eyes, and tried to sleep.

CHAPTER 14

A FEW HOURS LATER, PRESLEY REALIZED HE'D MANAGED TO surprise her.

She'd been prepared to be charmed by his charisma and sharp wit, but it was the other stuff that threw her off. The way he seemed to share things with her about his childhood, opening up about his struggle to find his place within the family dynamics. The way he listened to her suggestions to make his brewery more environmentally friendly, and even jotting down notes on his phone regarding places to donate unused grain and put in better recycling methods. His pointed questions and obvious fascination with her opinions and beliefs puzzled her. He seemed hungry for all the knowledge he could gain from her. She averted the questions that would hint at their shared past, and took advantage, learning his weak spots and likes that she could use to further her attempts to get him to fall for her. She was sure she'd remain laser-focused on the end goal of her entire game plan.

Unfortunately, she forgot completely about the plan and fell under Nolan Banks' spell.

Again.

The biggest shocker of all, though?

He hadn't kissed her.

Oh, he'd technically kissed her, but it totally didn't count. It was a barely there touch, one that shouldn't have had her body roaring with want or her panties dampening in need. Yet, it still rocked her pathetic world.

She'd expected body slamming, tongue plunging, and erotic kissing. His hormones and male aura had been practically raging with sexual frustration, mirroring her own unfulfilled desire. It was what she'd expected Nolan Banks to do—the man who wanted a hot body underneath him. But the gentle kiss and sweet way he'd smiled at her afterward had *not* been expected.

Bastard.

By the end of the dinner, her head was spinning and her center of gravity had been firmly tilted. "I know I mentioned it before but I'm holding the soft launch for The Bank on Saturday night. I'd love for you to come," he said, refilling her water and wine glasses automatically before the server could even reach their table.

Presley realized she had to pull back and regroup for a moment. It was time to get back to the seductive, cool persona that would snag and keep his interest. She'd slipped into her real self during dinner and forgotten to play her role. That wasn't the type of woman who'd thrill and seduce him. He'd already proven he wasn't interested in the real her—the one at the party who'd been open with her heart and ready to give him whatever he asked freely and happily. When Presley finally fell for a man, she wanted to know she'd be safe whether she was a size 22 or a size 12.

She gave a slow smile and stretched, making sure her bare legs were kicked out in front of him as a distraction. "I'm sure it'll be fabulous, but I'm unable to commit yet as I may have plans."

Funny, he didn't look at her legs this time. His gaze focused on her face. "Are you seeing anyone else, Presley?" he asked seriously.

She hesitated, wondering what the right answer was. Did he like the elusive type or would he prefer to win her for himself? Probably the latter. Men were a bit possessive. "No, I'm casually dating but not seeing anyone in a relationship."

His body relaxed. "Good. If you can't make it Saturday, I'd love to take you to dinner another night. Friday?"

She gave a tinkly laugh and rubbed his arm in a practiced gesture. "How sweet. Why don't you call me and we'll see what happens?"

She knew men loved a good challenge and the chase. It was the perfect answer. Satisfied, she reached for her purse, ready to make a handy dash to the ladies' room. Before she could exit, he leaned forward, a frown creasing his brow, as an inquisitive look formed on his face that questioned her coy approach, almost as he could see the real Presley behind the mask she tried to wear. "Did you have a good time with me tonight?"

She blinked. "Yes."

"So, did I. In fact, I can't remember the last time I enjoyed a woman's company so much." His voice rang with truth and threw her off. He reached out and snagged her hand, entwining his fingers with hers. "I think you know I'm attracted to you. I want to see you again."

The words pierced through her, bringing crushing pain. She'd gotten caught up in the image he portrayed along with his caring words and intimate looks. But like a beautiful, shiny apple that's seductive to the eye and tempting with sweetness, inside he was rotten. How could he forget that night? How else could he do something like that to her and not have regret? How many other women had he hurt?

She couldn't help the hard bitterness encrusted within her words. "I'm flattered you feel that way."

He quirked a brow. "Doesn't seem so. Did I say something wrong?"

She shrugged and tried to pull her hand back. He refused. "What woman on the planet doesn't want to hear she's attractive and wanted by a charming man?"

"This is more than that. There's something about you that draws me to you, a force I know you feel too. I think we both know there's something between us."

The snarl almost escaped her lips. "Yes, sexual attraction. You like my body and I like yours. You find me desirable on a physical level as I do you. I know exactly what's between us."

His frown deepened. She was furious at herself for craving to lift her hand and touch him, smoothing it away, tracing the line of that scar that had fascinated her since college. To be the woman to earn the right to touch him like that was a yearning in her very soul, and it'd only been one short evening in his company that already shattered all her walls and barriers she'd carefully built over the years.

She needed an escape strategy before she blew this whole thing up. Presley forced a smile. "Dinner was amazing, but we better go. I have an early morning meeting."

"Not until we clear a few things up." His gaze gripped her in a fierce embrace, glowing with a fiery blue light. "I'm not going to lie and tell you I wasn't affected by your appearance. Yes, I'm sexually attracted to you. Yes, my body nearly buckled with the need to touch you, kiss you, make you shatter in my arms. I sure as hell am not going to apologize for feeling all those things. But it's more than that. I've been sexually attracted to women many times, but never experienced a real connection. Like there's a fuse between us that lights up when we get near each other. My body's not just excited, Presley. My mind is. And God knows, if we keep moving in this direction, even though I may scare the living hell out of you, my heart may just follow. How's that for truth?"

Stunned, she stared back at him, unable to form a response. *This was exactly what she wanted.* Just one date and he thought he was falling for her. Hell, she gave it one good making out session with blue balls, and another date where she dazzled him, and she'd be ready to reveal her truth and great revenge.

Instead, raw emotions chopped through her like riding out a stormy sail. What would it be like to erase the past and allow herself to believe he was beginning to care for the true woman inside? To allow them a second chance based on truth rather than lies? To stop playing this game and just get real? She could tell him everything right now and be prepared for the fall-out. She could finally confront him about his actions and see where they navigated, or if it was even possible.

But the old fear and insecurity reared up and reminded her one important thing.

No matter how much he denied it, Nolan was intrigued by her looks. Her fake charm. Her calculated wit. Her wardrobe and her body. She'd used them as weapons, and they'd worked. There was only one recourse.

Follow it to the end and expose him.

Presley ducked her head, buying herself time. "I'm over-whelmed, Nolan," she said softly. "I won't lie and tell you I don't feel all those things with you. But I need to be sure. I need to go slow. Do you understand?"

He tipped her chin up, forcing her to look at him while holding her breath as she tried to hide the truth and present him with what he wanted to see. Seconds beat by. Then slowly, he nodded, and a smile tipped his lips. "I'm sorry. I swear I'm never that intense on a first date. Let's just say you've managed to surprise me."

Her shoulders sagged with relief. "Back atcha, beer man."

The energy lightened, and they fell back into the easy cama-raderie of dinner. He paid the bill, and they drove back to Port Hudson. They got into a lively discussion over music—he was rock and roll and she was country, baseball teams—he was Yankees and she was Mets, and favored pets—he was dogs, and she was cats. They did agree on politics, climate change, books, and that *Game of Thrones* was the best series ever created, with *Sons of Anarchy* as a close second.

By the time he pulled up to her home, as he'd refused to drop her off in front of her work building, Presley once again had to remind herself to properly play the game and not be distracted by his sexy charm. What were the rules her friends had specified again?

Be Mean. Play hard to get. Seduce. Use humor. Leave him wanting more.

She mentally ticked off all the ones she'd accomplished. Good, she'd managed to succeed in almost all areas. But the most important was about to happen right now. She needed to make sure she left him wanting more, but before she could do that, one vital question must be answered.

Kiss or no kiss?

"Let me walk you to the door," he said, climbing out of the car and opening her door. This time, his hand lay warmly over the small of her back, his fingers pressing against her bare skin. Shivers of pleasure raced down her spine, and her heart rapped madly inside her chest in slight panic. What was she going to do? If she kissed him, would it be too soon? The kiss at dinner had been just a tease, and maybe if she amped up her game, he'd leave with his dick messing with his head. But if she didn't kiss him, maybe it would be the ultimate challenge and drive him mad with wanting.

"Your home is charming," he said, his husky voice rumbling in the shadows. The solar lights illuminated the curving cobblestone pathway leading up to the stone cottage. She could have built a mansion or lived in a fancy building with all amenities, but the moment she spied the cottage, she'd known it was meant for her. It reminded her of a fairy tale, with ivy creeping up the front, surrounded by thick trees and dark woods and wildflowers. The quirky sloped red roof was angled sharply, and the windows were off center, but it had a magical appeal as if sprites visited daily, playing in the lush garden as they danced by the bubbling brook that snaked over to the right side.

"Thank you."

He reached her door but he didn't drop his hand. "It suits you."

She moved away from his grip, even though her body raged against the decision. "How do you know?" she asked curiously.

He shrugged, but the gesture seethed with meaning. "You're a powerful, savvy woman who runs her world exactly as she wants to. But behind that perfect exterior, there's a heart and soul of a true romantic. A woman who loves romance novels and charming cottages but also a good-old fashioned steak. Not to mention an underdog story. Why else would you be a Mets fan?"

His teasing softened the intensity of his words, but she was still struck by his realizations. He was too close to the truth, and she took another step back, desperately needing the distance. "Men do adore a good mystery," she said, trying to tease back. "Wouldn't want to bore you on the first date."

A crease furrowed his brow. "That would never be your problem, Presley Cabot," he said softly. "The bigger issue would be having a man try to forget you."

Like he forgot her?

A throbbing ache hit her. This was the second time he'd uttered such a statement, and the second time he proved he was a good liar. He'd forgotten everything about her, but he liked his pretty words and his romantic gestures. She pulled herself to full height of 5'8, shoulders back, head up, and looked him straight in the eye. No, this date would end without a kiss. This was a man who'd prefer a more difficult challenge in order to remember. "I guess we'll see then, won't we?"

The hook was perfect. She gave a slow, seductive smile, and pivoted on her heel, stepping to the safety of her door.

"You did it again."

She stiffened at his sudden words. Turned to glance back. "Excuse me?"

Head cocked, he studied her with intensity, as if trying to figure out a secret. "One moment, you're completely connected to me. It's like you're open so I can really see you. Then you pull back and do a one-eighty. Completely change. I can't figure it and you out yet."

A laugh escaped her lips, but it fell flat. "You can't expect everything in one night, Nolan. It doesn't work like that."

"I know." He stepped closer, his face tight with intention. "But you don't have to hide with me. I want to get to know who you really are."

Retreat, the voice inside her screamed. *Get the hell back behind the front door and try again tomorrow.*

She couldn't help the touch of irritation in her voice. "Isn't that what they all say? Is it so easy for you to put yourself out there? Or are you just pretending to show it all and be vulnerable when you're really locked behind your own glass wall, an insular effect that allows you to be protected because there's no real connection? Good-night, Nolan."

Let him ponder her cryptic words. Hopefully, it'd keep him up at night. She began to turn away again, but suddenly he jerked hard, a haunted, searching look glittering in his blue eyes. "What did you say?" he asked in urgency, leaning toward her. "About a glass wall separating you?"

She sighed impatiently. "It's just something I term the insular eff—" she stopped herself, horror unfolding as she watched the memory flicker, as if his mind was frantically searching to find the missing thread of her statement. Was it possible he was remembering their conversation so long ago?

"I've heard that before," he muttered in a low voice, shaking his head. "This is so weird, I swear someone I knew told me about that. It's so familiar."

"Oh, it was probably in a short story from school," she threw out, trying not to sound desperate. "Faulkner, or Dickens, or—"

"No, this was someone I knew, wait a minute, I think—"

Panicking, she jumped into his arms, trying to distract him from the truth.

Obviously stunned from her sudden move, he stumbled back but managed to catch her. His hands cupped her butt and her held her flush against his chest, as Presley slammed her mouth toward his, hoping for the big romantic gesture where their lips meet and everything else seeps out of their mind except each other and the glittering, perfect moment.

Except it was her life.

First, her teeth gnashed against his and hurt like a mother, until he groaned in pain and pulled back. But then her center of gravity slipped and she clawed frantically at him. Instead of grabbing onto his shoulders, she made contact with his hair, pulling at it in a way that was more BDSM than sexy. But the worst was the awful sound of tearing fabric as she tried to wrap her legs around his hips (She'd always dreamed of doing it against a wall but it never seemed to work for her) but instead ripped open the seams of her priceless, custom dress and felt the sudden rush of air over her black lace underwear.

He grunted hard, taking a few steps backward, trying to keep her safely off the ground, but it was too late.

His heel got caught on a paver and he fell.

He hit the ground, she hit his chest full force, and they both fell over onto the damp grass.

For a few seconds, she closed her eyes and hoped the entire episode had been one of those flash dreams of what could have happened, but really didn't.

But it had.

Game over.

CHAPTER 15

NOLAN HIT THE GROUND HARD.

His breath whooshed out of his lungs, and he was a bit humiliated to admit he may have turned his ankle a bit on the way down, which was not a very manly impression to make to the woman who'd jumped in his arms for a kiss.

Of course, that move had been quite unexpected.

His teeth hurt a bit from the crash of her teeth, but he'd loved the enthusiasm, which had taken him by stunned surprise. He stared up at the twinkling stars in the night sky, and finally managed to get in a lungful of air. It was then he noticed the warm, curvy weight of woman currently cradled tight in his arms. Well, arm. His other one was pinned against something deliciously warm, and wet and—

The realization hit him like a hurtling freight train.

Holy shit. His hand was pressed against her lace clad pussy. From under her dress? But it didn't feel like there was any fabric between them unless—

Yep. Half the dress was hanging to the side, torn completely off, and baring those amazing legs to his view. But his hand ...

Oh, God, his hand.

He couldn't help but automatically stroke a bit, the scratch of lace damp and so exquisitely sexy his brain just blanked out completely. Unbelievably, her hips flexed, bringing him even closer, his thumb pressed right over the hard button of her clit that seemed to be begging for some attention he desperately wanted to give. A feminine moan broke through, and she shifted on his chest, her head coming up to look him foggily in the eyes.

"I think I moved too fast," she said a bit sheepishly, blinking those amazing eyes that pierced through the surface and into his soul. "Are you hurt?"

Yes. He hurt all over, from a pure aching to get his hands and tongue all over her naked body. "No. I'm sorry, I should have caught you better." He tried hard to move his hand away, he really did, but it was like his hand had a mind of its own and brushed over her hard clit.

"Oh." Her breath caught and her teeth sunk into her lush bottom lip. She wriggled closer and a torturous moan vibrated in his throat. She was so damn sexy. And yes, he was an asshole because he did it again. Pink flushed her cheeks, and his fingers were deliciously damp with her arousal. "Nolan?" His name broke on a question. A plea. A demand.

His blood boiled with raw need. He used his other arm to grip the back of her head and he yanked her tight against him. Her breath came in choppy gasps and he ached to swallow every single one. His gaze locked on hers. "Kiss me, Presley. Finish what you started."

He gave her one second to pull back.

She didn't.

Then his lips were on hers.

She kissed him back.

Shocking, sexual heat roared through him at the first full frontal body contact, mouth-to-mouth, hip-to-hip, breasts-to-chest. Her lips opened easily, her tongue sliding into his mouth to welcome and play. Drinking in the taste of sweet wine, green tea and exotic, feminine spice, he murmured in primitive satisfaction, the ground beneath him shifting and whirling like he'd gone on a bender and couldn't find his center of gravity.

She exploded in his arms, her soft, firm weight filling up every inch of his space, driving every other thought and need from his mind except the demand to pleasure, satisfy, and claim. He took the kiss deeper like a starved man, reveling in every slick, damp inch of her gorgeous mouth. His hand slid under the elastic of her panties—all bets off—and dove into tight, dripping heat. Holy crap, she was so damn wet for him, her pussy clenching around his finger in desperate need for more. Teasing her clit, he curled his fingers and thrust deeper, crazed to make her shatter and come all over his hand.

She cried out, her teeth sinking into his lip, her hips rolling helplessly under the play of his magical fingers that stroked her like a keyboard, each touch making her pleasure-induced sounds louder.

"You're burning up in my arms," he groaned, rubbing and rotating his palm over her hot core. "God, I can't get enough of you. Let me make you feel good, sweetheart."

He wanted to hear his name on her lips as she screamed; to drive inside of her with his cock with no barriers between them. A primitive, possessive energy surged through him, and he knew in that shattering moment, this woman owned a part of him already after only one night.

He'd do anything to make her his.

The faint sound of an alarm shrieking in the quiet night told him fate had a cruel sense of humor. Suddenly, she stiffened above him, those blue-gray eyes widening as sanity began to trickle into their sensual world. Nolan cursed under his breath and said good-bye to bestowing an orgasm to this amazing woman. At least for tonight.

Slowly, he removed his hand from underneath her dress, already mourning the sweet sultriness of her body. The entire episode seemed to hit her all at once, because suddenly she leapt off his body and gathered her torn dress around her. "I have to go."

He rolled to his feet, his hands up in a surrender gesture. "Do you want to talk about it?"

"No! Hell, no, I want to get inside, thanks. For dinner! Not that—bye!"

In seconds, she'd scurried inside and slammed the door behind her.

Well, fuck. That hadn't gone as well as he expected.

Nolan made his way back to the car, still rock-hard from a night that quickly went from scorching hot to unexpectedly not. She was such a puzzle. One moment, she was a cool seductress who made him want to drop to his knees. Her razor wit and ballsy comments attacked his ego, which had been fed way too much in his past relationships. If he could even call them relationships. More like weekly night stands. His average commitment ranged in the month category, and that was because he didn't believe in using women to scratch an itch and then walk away. He wouldn't mind a partner in life. A beautiful and brainy woman by his side, his equal, someone to weather the good and the bad, and see him for what was beneath his façade.

But Presley was so much more than a challenge.

It was the woman he spotted lurking beneath the polished temptress that he was desperate to unveil. The one who peeked out when she didn't think he was looking—the woman who jumped into his arms and ripped her dress—and then argued passionately for environmental reform while she shared intimate things about how she saw the world. The combination was complete intoxication. Presley was complete intoxication.

Nolan drove away, whistling under his breath. Life was good. He was about to open up the bar of his dreams, and he'd met a woman of his dreams, the one who may change his future.

Damn, he couldn't wait to see her again.

CHAPTER 16

W HEN P RESLEY WOKE UP, HER HEAD THROBBED AND HER BODY ACHED.
*It took her a few minutes to remember where she was and what had
happened last night. She sucked in a breath and turned.*

He was asleep beside her.

*He'd held her most of the night. When she awoke in a panic, the
strong, comforting weight of his body reminded her she was safe. She'd
hoped they could make love again, but he'd been in a deep slumber,
obviously exhausted.*

*She stared at the ceiling, smiling. Every image was imprinted in
her memory. Her fantasy had finally come true.*

Nolan Banks had taken her virginity.

*The echo of laughter and talk filled the air. Ugh, his frat brothers
were up. This was the awkward part she wasn't prepared for—doing
the walk of shame right in front of them.*

*Frowning, she checked the clock and groaned. God, how was it ten
AM already? She had to get out of here—Aubrey and Libby were
probably freaking out.*

This time, when she pulled away, Nolan didn't budge. Wincing at her sore muscles, she got her phone, scrolling through her friend's texts, and punched out her response.

Everything great. Coming home soon.

Now she had to get into the bathroom without being seen. She quickly got dressed, eased open the door, and peeked her head out. Noises still came from the kitchen, so she quickly headed down the hall and into the bathroom, locking it behind her.

With a sigh of relief, she took a few minutes to rub some toothpaste over her teeth, finger comb her crazy hair, and straighten up her clothes. When she peed, she was relieved to see no bleeding. Good. She was one of the lucky ones. Finally, she felt ready enough to go out there. She'd just smile nicely, say good morning, and race straight out the front door. She was sure Nolan's frat group had seen plenty of females walk out in the morning.

No big deal.

Presley left the bathroom and paused before Nolan's door. Should she try to say goodbye first or just disappear? This was so confusing. Probably better to leave him asleep. Just in case he—

The fractured pieces of conversation rose from the kitchen and snagged her attention.

"Always wanted to do a fat girl," a voice said, laughing. "They're supposed to tear up the sheets and give good head."

"Yeah, heard that, too. Desperate for love," another male voice said. "But didn't know Nolan was into that. He seems to favor skinny blondes."

"Variety is the spice of life, man. He bet me last night he could get her into bed without a hitch. Bastard didn't even have to work that hard. She couldn't wait to bang the golden boy."

More laughter. "Hey, if he says she's good, maybe I'll give her a turn."

CHAPTER 17

"OH MY GOD, THOSE FLOWERS ARE GORGEOUS!"

Libby gave a deep sigh and stuck her nose in the middle of the explosion of blooms, smiling with pleasure. Aubrey gave the bouquet an assessing long stare, as if it was really a bomb she was thinking about disarming. Presley groaned and banged her head on the desk.

"I don't get it. Last night was a nightmare. Yet, he's still interested."

Aubrey snorted and dropped in her favorite chair. "His hand was in your hoo ha. Of course he's still interested. Did you tell Cam you ruined his dress?"

"No! I'm going to try and get it fixed before he kills me."

"Nah, if you got Nolan all hot and bothered, he'll consider the outfit a success."

Libby laughed, going over to the table to grab a cup of coffee. "Maybe he found your antics charming?" she suggested.

"He'd be crazy not to want you, Pres. You only had one date and he's already tied up in knots."

"You think?" she asked doubtfully, picking her head back up. "Is that the pecan butter flavor coffee I like?"

"Yes, I'll bring you a cup," Libby said.

"Thanks, babe." She smiled at her friend.

"What does the card say?" Aubrey asked.

She'd already memorized it, reading the scrawling, messy script over and over. Presley tried not to blush as she recited it. "Every date with us should end with you in my arms. Thinking of you."

Libby sighed. "Beautiful."

"Oh, he's good," Aubrey said. "You have him on the ropes, Pres! It's almost time to close in for the big finale."

Presley tried to ignore the sudden lurch of nausea. Why did the idea of confronting him now scare the hell out of her? Before, she only burned for a sense of justice and revenge. Now, after only one date, she was already waffling about the entire plan. "He invited me to the soft launch of The Bank Saturday night. I told him I may have plans."

Aubrey tapped her fingers against the smooth red leather. "I think you should go, but not with him. Just show up and surprise him. He needs to be kept off kilter at all times."

Libby handed her the coffee, her face set into concerned lines. "Did you enjoy the date with him?" she asked.

Aubrey's gaze swiveled over and pinned her with a stare.

She took a sip of coffee to buy more time. Had she? Hell, yes. It had been one of her best dates, which pissed her off. She tried to remind herself it was all fake on his part, and she wouldn't let Nolan pull her back into his world, but she couldn't stop thinking about him. She'd enjoyed every minute of the date so much she'd forgotten the end game. Enjoyed his beautiful body and mind; his wit and humor. Enjoyed his magical mouth and hands that almost made her body scream the big 'O. Enjoyed the way his fingers had stroked and pleasured and--

"Oh, my God!" Aubrey yelled, jumping up from the chair. "It's happening again! You're falling for him."

"Am not!" she yelled back.

"You're blushing," Libby pointed out with a sigh. "That's not a good sign."

"It's hot in here," she muttered, turning away from her friends. "Look, I have everything under control. I'll show up at his launch and seal the deal."

"Don't sleep with him, Pres," Aubrey warned, shaking her finger. "He's pond scum. Just get him all riled up, make him beg, then tell him you wouldn't sleep with him if he was the last man on earth. It'll feel amazing and you can finally close this chapter. Right?"

"Right," she said strongly, nodding. "I got this.

"No sex," Libby emphasized.

Presley shot them both a glare. "I got it, okay! I don't even want to have sex with him. Yuck."

Aubrey rolled her eyes. Libby looked even more concerned.

"Guys, stop worrying and meddling. I need to get back to work."

They finally left, leaving her alone in her office with the smell of wildflowers. She leaned over and took an appreciative sniff. How did he know she adored the type of seeds that sprouted in the most rugged environment, rising from the rocks and rubble to sprout in happy colors and messy blooms?

Those dignified hothouse flowers bored her to tears. There was nothing hearty underneath.

Worry twisted her insides. She had to keep the wall up for a little longer. The end would justify the means, right? After all, she'd fantasized about getting even with the one man who'd destroyed her. He deserved it, *didn't he?*

She'd be distant this week. Cool, yet a bit flirty. She'd refuse to see him, which would keep him off kilter. Maybe just a text or two to hold him on the hook. She'd follow Aubrey's advice and make excuses regarding the soft launch, then just show up.

The plan was still perfect. She just had to finish it before he finished her.

She kept repeating the mantra throughout the day, even though the words were beginning to sound a bit hollow.

Nolan tilted the pint glass and poured the Port Hudson draft he'd been perfecting for the last few months. The sharp tang of grapefruit mixed with the earthiness of pine for a balance he was proud of. He'd experimented with the hops and ended up using Amarillo, which gave him the lasting flavor without too much bitterness. So far, the crowd loved it, along with his Summer Ale, an easy citrus with just a touch of tart to take it up a notch.

He slid the beer across the bar and scanned the crowd one more time.

She wasn't coming.

He tried to smother the trickle of disappointment and concentrated on his first launch party. His chef's tasting platters were a big hit, and the back room was lively with games of pool and darts amidst some good old-fashioned rock music playing in the background. Only two hours in, and he'd already deemed it a complete success.

Except that Presley hadn't showed.

He'd called and texted after sending the flowers, hoping she'd agree to another date. She texted back once, citing her busy schedule, and had an actual conversation with him via phone, where she was cool, flirty, and extremely maddening. He mentioned the party again, and she told him she'd try but couldn't make any promises. The opening was taking all his extra time so he'd had no chance this week to try and track her down, or wait in her office, hoping she'd see him.

It was official. He was pathetic. Acting like a trained puppy, he was completely whipped and under the spell of a woman who could just be playing games with him, or eventually break his heart. He couldn't stop thinking about the kiss and how she practically blazed to life in his arms. How it had seemed so honest and pure.

He sensed there was something more to her that had elicited this strong pull of familiarity or maybe even fate. When he gazed into those blue-gray eyes, something shifted inside of him, like he'd found his missing piece. As if he was just picking up where he'd left off.

Obviously, she didn't feel the same.

He was falling apart and maybe making a fool out of himself. Crap, he was trapped in a Taylor Swift song and if anyone knew, he'd be tortured for the rest of his life. He should just turn in his man card because his balls now seem to be owned by Presley.

On cue, his brother's voice rose to his ears.

"I've had piss that tasted better than this."

He looked up, grinning back at Carter as he held a pint glass high, pretending to examine the color. His brother may give him crap, and be ruthless with competition, but Nolan knew he'd left his own bar at peak time to support him.

"Good, it'll go with the crappy burger you served me the other day. Do people actually pay a ton more for your deluxe platter just to get some wilted lettuce and a tomato?"

His brother laughed. With his curly brown hair and blue eyes, he was pretty much his twin, just older. Nolan loved rubbing that in his face. "Asshole. How's it going?"

He wiped up the bar and took another round of beer orders. "Good. People seem to like the brews, and the tasting menu is going to put you out of business."

"You wish, little bro. Talk to Mom and Dad?"

Nolan nodded. "They're coming for the official launch but I told him not to bother tonight."

"Heard Landon made a shitload of money on the Patterson Tech deal. She's got the shark instinct. Think she'll stay?"

Nolan thought about his sister immersed in the cutthroat world of finance. "Don't know. She's not like most girls—she hates talking about her feelings. When I try to ask if she's happy, she just gives me that grunt."

"Yeah. Maybe we can get her to come to Port Hudson and open up a wine bar."

Nolan laughed. "Who would've thought alcohol was our Yellow Brick Road?"

"Yeah. Speaking of which, remember when you peed your pants when the flying monkeys came on the screen? Had nightmares for days and begged to sleep in Mom's bed."

He opened his mouth to tell his brother to fuck off, but to his horror, another voice cut in. A sexy, throaty, familiar voice.

"Personally, the talking trees who threw apples always freaked me out."

No. No, no, no...

He lifted his gaze and collided with amused gray eyes. She gave him a wink and slid into the stool next to his brother. As humiliating as her entrance was, his heart leapt in his chest at her presence, and he knew he was in big trouble.

"Hey, Carter. Here to torture your little brother on opening night?"

"It's a soft launch," Carter grunted. "Good to see you, Pres. Got a hot date later? You're all sexied up."

This time, she was the one who blushed, but Nolan was too freaked out by his brother's familiar greeting. Holy shit, what if they'd dated in the past? It was a small town, and Carter had been here a while. Nolan hadn't told him about their date or his feelings. Had they been more than casual friends?

Presley waved her hand in the air. "I'm in jeans and a tank. Definitely no date tonight."

Temper roared through him. He placed his hands on the bar and leaned over.

"How well do you two know each other?" he demanded.

Carter jerked and shot him a look. "What do you mean? She comes to eat at Quarters, usually with her friends. Why, you guys dating or something?"

"No," Presley shot back.

"Yes," he said, his voice firm. "We're dating."

"Take it down a notch, beer man," she drawled, crossing her jean clad legs and propping her elbow on the bar. A slight smile played on her lips. She looked calm and controlled under his brother's curious stare. "Can I try the Port Hudson please?"

He grabbed a glass, tilted it, and poured the draft. "We went to dinner," he pointed out. "Plus, I sent you flowers. I'd classify that as dating."

"I'd classify it as eating one meal together."

"I asked you to be my date tonight and you're here."

She lifted the glass and considered him over the rim. Then licked her lips in anticipation. "I never formally accepted your date," she said. "I'm here all on my own."

Carter whistled. "This is getting intense, dudes. And as fascinating as this dialogue is with all that crankin' sexual tension, I think I'll go play some darts."

His brother picked up his beer and disappeared into the crowd.

Nolan never broke eye contact. Just watched her sip his brew, enjoying the quick dart of pleasure that flickered over her face. She liked it. Pride surged that he'd been able to please her.

He intended to please her for many, many hours and in many, many ways.

Soon.

"I don't like the jealous type," she announced, tapping her nails against the pint glass. "Or the pushy type."

"I'm not either. But the idea of you kissing my brother and enjoying it drives me out of my fucking mind."

She jerked, meeting his gaze. The current of energy sizzled between them. Her pupils darkened, and her lips parted slightly to puff out a breath.

Right there. There was the woman who gave him an honest reaction and proved she was just as into him as he was with her. He had to go with his instincts. Something was blocking her from letting him in. A past hurt? A broken relationship? Trust issues?

It could be anything. The world was cruel in its doling out

of pain, and the idea of her suffering at some asshole's hands hurt his heart. He needed to be patient and let her run when she needed to. Nolan would just be right there when she came back.

"I never went out with your brother," she said softly.

"Thank you, for telling me that, and for coming tonight. Do you like the beer?"

"Yes. It has a fabulous mingling of grapefruit and spice. Hops are well balanced and smooth. What is the other flavor I'm sensing? Blood-orange."

"Very good." Satisfaction flowed. "If you want one day, I'll show you how I brew a batch."

For a few seconds, the mask dropped, and she smiled back tentatively. "I'd like that."

Someone called his name, and he excused himself to pour more beer, and accept more congratulations. But for the rest of the evening, all his attention was focused on the mysterious Presley Cabot, and how he could keep her beautiful ass perched on his barstool.

CHAPTER 18

PRESLEY KNEW THE HARDEST PART WOULD BE SEEING NOLAN IN English class.

She'd seriously considered dropping it and taking the failing grade, but Aubrey and Libby convinced her otherwise. They'd been ready to kick some serous ass and storm the frat house, but her frantic begs to keep the silence finally resonated.

She refused to go through further humiliation. She only wanted the whole episode to vanish from her memory and pretend she'd never had sex with Nolan Banks. If only there was a pill invented to forget about bad decisions or events. Instead, she'd decided to pretend the entire episode had never occurred. If she gave him no indication he meant anything to her, maybe her humiliation would be lessened. It was the only play she had left.

He arrived late to class so she didn't have any torturous, dead time to suffer through. Thank God, most of the class was focused on working on their own separate writing pieces, and she managed to concentrate on her story. Of course, she was aware of him the entire time. Endless months spent obsessing over his every moment and memorizing every detail of his physical presence couldn't be eroded in a few days. Still, she tried, refusing to look over, and finally she was free.

She'd grabbed her folders and purse, stuffing her pens inside, and managed to get through the door when she heard her name.

Automatically, she froze, her heart beating madly against her ribcage in an attempt to be freed. In slow motion, she glanced back and watched him walk toward her, that gorgeous smile on his face. "Hey, how are you doing? Tough assignment today, huh? I mean, who really cares what our earliest memory is. Kind of a waste."

Her tongue stuck to the roof of her mouth. Rage burned deep in her gut, but it was the other emotion that made everything so much worse. The way her body still remembered him, the way her pathetic heart yearned for him to explain everything and make it all nice again. But that was a lie, and maybe it was time she began living with the truth.

So, instead of answering, she stared back at him and remained silent, refusing to acknowledge what he obviously chose to forget.

He shifted his weight. A slight frown creased his brow. "Umm, did you have a good time at the party?"

"Did you?" she shot back, her voice encrusted with ice.

"Yeah. Hey, is something wrong? You're acting weird."

She couldn't help the words from tumbling out of her mouth, like acid on her tongue. "I know about the bet."

Surprise flickered over his face. He groaned and rubbed his forehead. "Ah, crap, you weren't supposed to know about that. I'm sorry. I had too much to drink and got carried away, I guess." He guessed?

The events of the night whipped before her in all its mockery. Suddenly, a tornado of emotions hit her, and she closed the distance between them, head tilted up to meet his gaze face to face. "You bastard," she whispered in a shaky voice. "Let's get one thing straight. I think you're a piece of shit. You've had everything handed to you and never had to fight for anything you wanted. You treat people like they're disposable. You're a waste of space and not even worth my time. Don't look at me, don't talk to me, and don't come near me or I'll make you regret it."

He jerked back, eyes widened with shock. "Presley, wait. I'm really sorry, I—"

"Just stay the hell away."

This time, she forced her feet to move. His gaze burned into her back until she turned the corridor and got lost in the chattering chaotic crowd, and swore she'd never think of Nolan Banks ever again.

CHAPTER 19

"Can I drive you home?"

Presley shook her head, walking around the now empty space. "I have my car and I only had one beer."

"One and a half," he corrected. He was frowning again, that adorable concerned look on his face. Curly brown hair flopped over his brow. "I'd feel better if you stayed a bit longer. Had a cup of coffee."

She smiled in amusement. "Is this your way to lure me into your lair, beer man?" she teased.

"I wouldn't forgive myself if something happened to you," he said simply.

Why did he have to care?

The truth of his words cut through the shadowed dark and wrapped them in intimacy. She cleared her throat and turned her back, desperately seeking composure. What was happening to her? When had her ruthless control slipped out of her grasp? When had he begun to soften her traitorous heart? What made her want to ditch her revenge plan? Or more like *who* because Nolan was slowly seeping into her heart.

Each time she saw him, another chink of her armor broke off. It was easier to believe he just wanted to sleep with her for a challenge, but all evidence was pointing in another direction. A direction she couldn't believe in and one she was not sure she could navigate.

He seemed to like her.

They'd only had one brief conversation on the phone since their date, but it was memorable. He asked her questions, seeming interested in her work and daily routine. Tonight, even though he was supposed to be at the beck and call of new customers, he'd focused on her, making sure she was engaged in conversations, and proudly claiming her as his official date of the evening.

He was fun and flirty but worst of all, he seemed real. Like he was putting everything out there in the quest for....

For what? A relationship? A short affair? A few nights of great sex?

It was getting harder to play the game and pretend. He may be a liar, but she was still weak in his presence. Her body wept, her soul longed, and her mind puzzled out the mystery, wanting to believe he'd changed, and they could be *more*.

But they couldn't. Because he'd hurt, humiliated, and destroyed her.

Because she'd been fat and forgettable.

It was time to finish this and get back to her regular life. Close the door once and for all on the past and the misty, distant future that did not contain Nolan Banks.

Pivoting on her heel, she shot him a slow, seductive smile. "Maybe you're right. Coffee sounds good." She paused, letting the anticipation build. Did a little wriggle to show off her butt in the tight Guess jeans. "Don't you live close by?"

He stilled. Like a wolf scenting prey, his nostrils flared and a shiver of excitement raced down her spine. Nothing would happen, of course. She was just going to tease him a bit. Maybe share a kiss. Then pull away and inform him exactly why she despised him.

"Yeah, right up the block." He cocked a hip and raked his gaze over her figure. "You want to go to my place?"

"Do you have good coffee?" she drawled.

An arrogant smile touched his lips. "I have the best."

She quirked a brow in challenge and gave a low laugh. "Prove it."

A low growl rumbled from his throat. "I intend to. Let's go."

He grabbed his keys, switched off the rest of the lights, and led her outside.

The walk was short. He took her hand, his grip warm and strong, and they strolled in silence. With every step, the tension inside her grew tighter, but she pushed it aside, sure of her plan. His house was a white cape cod with black shutters, a large yard, and a small porch where a bunch of mismatched rockers and tables scattered about. A giant weeping willow tree bent gracefully over an old swing set. A grill and fire pit took up the side lawn.

She followed him inside, curiously taking in her surroundings. The entire home pulsed with comfort and familiarity, definitely masculine but with touches of thoughtfulness. His main room held leather recliners, a huge sectional, and a few ottomans as if he invited his friends over every Sunday for football. The décor of Tuscan gold, rich reds, and neutrals gave it pop. The floors were a warm oak. Interesting paintings hung on the wall of the human body in the throes of motion—a runner breaking for the finish line, a skier jumping off the mountain, and a yogi holding a complicated pose. She shook her head at the elaborate Yankees sign, though even she had to grudgingly admit to liking the iconic, now retired Derek Jeter. The faint smell of cinnamon hung in the air, reminding her of fresh baked sticky buns.

"Let me put on the coffee," he said, kicking off his shoes on the front mat. "Get comfortable and I'll be right back."

He disappeared down the short hallway into the kitchen.

Presley pressed a trembling hand to her temple. Damnit, she needed to relax. He deserved none of her consideration after the way he'd treated her years ago. She dragged in a breath and wandered the living room, studying the many framed pictures of smiling family members and groups of friends. His bookshelf was crammed with an eclectic collection her fingers itched to browse through. An old phonograph sat on the table with an array of albums in classic rock. She plucked a worn one from the bottom of the pile. Billy Joel. Great choice.

Hard arms slid around her, easing her against his muscular chest. She breathed in the familiar smell of cotton, lemon, man, clean, and fresh in her nostrils. His nose nuzzled her neck, pushing her hair to the side so he could whisper in her ear. "Wanna hear a little *Piano Man?*" he asked, hands stroking over her hips. Even through her jeans, her skin burned, and her thighs softened, letting him work his magic.

"I thought you liked only the hard stuff."

His chuckle warmed her. He pressed a light kiss to the top of her shoulder and she couldn't hide her shiver. "Can't go hard all the time. We all need a little softness, don't you agree?"

He accented his words with tiny touches of his mouth,

working up the side of her neck, by her ear, over her cheek. So gentle and light, yet his hands pressed over her thighs, her ass, and her belly, as if hungry to touch her bare skin. She fought for focus, trying desperately to distract him. "We all hide one artist we don't want to admit to loving. What's yours?"

"I like *Le Miserables* the musical," he murmured. His tongue took a lazy path along the side of her jaw, then nibbled on the lobe of her ear. She had no idea her ears could be so damn sensitive. Sparks shot straight to her clit with each low spoken word. "And *Mama Mia.*"

She tried to pull away but her body refused to move. Her knees began to give way. "Stop teasing. How am I supposed to trust you if you won't tell me your secret musical weakness?"

He played with her fingers, traced her ribcage, and ever so slowly, wandered his way up to her breasts. Her tiny Swarovski beaded tank top was no match against the electric heat of his touch. Her breasts swelled and her nipples tightened, begging to be freed. She ached to have his mouth on her breasts, kissing, sucking, and giving pleasure. She was drowning slowly in a pool of lust along with a sea of sensation, and if she didn't battle her way out soon, Presley was afraid she'd never come back up for air.

"If I tell you, you have the power to blackmail me for life."

She arched back, wanting more of him, and he gave it to her. He ran the back of both palms over her straining nipples, the flimsy cotton fabric only emphasizing the erotic play. He growled and slowly pulled down the slinky straps over her shoulders. The fabric gave up with a pop, and she was suddenly bare-breasted, her back bowed like a gift she wanted to present for him to open.

"Tell me," she whispered, her voice husky with want.

"Barry Manilow."

She turned in his arms and looked into those deep sea-blue eyes. "That's hot."

Pure hunger carved out the lines of his face. Bending his head, he took one hard nipple in his mouth.

She cried out and succumbed to the sweet sensation, her body attuned to the moment. His mouth took her to heaven as he sucked, bit, and teased, while she pulled at his hair and lost herself in the embrace. The scrape of his teeth and the hot wetness of his tongue drove her mad, until she was unbuttoning his shirt with trembling fingers, frantic to feel him against her.

He shrugged off his shirt, and she ran her hands over the carved muscles of his chest, tugging at his hair, skimming over tight abs as she relished the way he jerked under her touch. He released her nipple and took her mouth in a deep, demanding kiss, his tongue thrusting while he backed her up against the sectional.

"Want you so bad," he gritted out, unsnapping her jeans and tugging them down over her hips. "Been dreaming about you every damn night. About this. Us."

The last word danced in her mind. Trying to shake off the sensual fog like a drunk attempting to pass a sobriety test, she barely grasped onto the edges of reality. "*Us?*" she repeated, his delicious taste lingering on her lips.

He dragged her close, her nipples pressing into the whorl of crisp hair and thighs bracing around his hips, the hard jut of his erection notched into her wet, needy channel, still blocked by her jeans. "Yes, us. This isn't a one-night thing for me, sweetheart. I'm kind of crazy about you." A self-conscious laugh spilled from his lips. Blinking in a daze, she gently touched that mouth she'd dreamed about, slowly working up his face to trace the mysterious scar that crisscrossed through his brow. "I'm not pushing or anything—we'll go at your pace. But it's important you know how I feel. I sense you've been holding back, and I know it's only been a damn week, and you get to have your barriers, but Presley, you need to know you're safe with me. I won't hurt you. I adore you."

She gazed into his eyes and saw he meant every word.

And then just like that—she was ripped back into the past. Walking past a group of jocks smirking, joking, and laughing about the track star bedding the fatty. The way he looked her dead in the face after class and told him he was sorry for the bet. Like it was no big deal. Like she was nothing.

Oh, no. Not this time.

Suddenly, everything crystalized into clarity, as the painful past reared its ugly head. She jerked back, fixing her jeans and her shirt with quick, furious movements. He blinked and took a step forward, frowning with concern. "Presley?"

"I'm safe with you, huh Nolan? I can trust you? I can show you everything I am and know you'll still care for me? Is that what you wanted to express?"

He rubbed his head, his narrowed gaze pinned to hers. He spoke in a calm voice. "Yes, that's exactly what I meant. We can go as slow or as fast as you want. I don't want to scare you. I just want you to know you're already important to me. I've never felt like this before."

"Bullshit," she shot back. "If I really meant something to you, you would've remembered me the first time we slept together."

His eyes widened with shock. "What the hell are you talking about? We never slept together before!"

Fury and ice whipped together for a poisonous cocktail. She

threw back her head and laughed, but there was no humor or emotion. "Guess my sexual skills weren't that memorable. Then again, neither was yours," she sneered.

A few beats passed. Temper seemed to hit and replace his confusion. "Okay, what game are you playing that I don't know about? I'm so lost here. Tell me what's going on, Presley."

"How does it feel, Nolan? To feel like you're safe—that you can open up and take a chance on someone? How does it feel to realize it's been a cruel lie, a joke, and that you meant nothing? Because that's what you did to me in college. At Boyer University. At that frat party you say you don't remember. When you slept with me and told your buddies you did it so you can experiment with the *fat girl*? Any of this sound familiar now, or are you going to stick to your story that you have no idea what I'm talking about?"

He opened his mouth, like he was about to yell, then suddenly snapped it closed. Shaking his head, he stumbled a few steps back. "Wait a minute. You went to Boyer? We met at a party? Wait—we hooked up?"

Her words were flung like cold, hard stones. "Yes. I wasn't stupid to believe we were going to live happily ever after like romance hero and heroines, but I thought you respected me. Wanted me. For God's sakes, we were in Professor Castle's class together and you even quoted my story."

Presley knew exactly when he remembered.

He jerked in horror, his shirt still hanging open, his features a mass of raw emotion as he seemed to try and piece together the past into the present. "Presley Cabot," he whispered hoarsely. "Dear God, that night. I met you in the bathroom, right? When Carl was sick. You were in my writing class, but I never put the two together because we barely spoke. And yes, I remember the story, the one about the glass barrier. That's what I was trying to remember Friday night."

"Yes. I wasn't ready for you to remember yet. I wanted to get you to this place, to this time, so you know what it feels like. To be betrayed. Humiliated." She blinked away the hot sting of tears from sheer anger. "To feel stupid for believing in something and someone."

He shoved his fingers through his hair. "I'm sorry I didn't remember. It's no excuse, but I'm horrible at names, and the professor called you Ms. Cabot. Other than the frat party, we'd never spoken before. But I do remember I liked you. I tried to talk to you the next day and you told me to get the hell away. I just figured you didn't like the way I was partying so I didn't think about it again."

Her breath whooshed out of her lungs. She spit out the words in fury. "Are you still telling me you don't remember the sex? How you took my virginity? How you slept with me just for a cruel bet?"

His head snapped around. His nostrils flared and he took a few steps forward. "I don't know what you're talking about. I never made a bet to sleep with you! Hell, I don't even remember that night I was partying so hard. I remember us talking in the bathroom, then chatting a bit in the kitchen, and then I didn't see you for the end of the night. Why would I make a bet to sleep with you?"

"Because I was fat!" she yelled. "I was fat and awkward, and had a terrible crush on you! I heard your stupid friends talking in the morning, Nolan. They were all laughing at the table about how you bet them you could get me into bed because fat girls know how to rock the sheets."

A sound came from his throat, but she was too far gone to

figure out what it was. The raw emotions tore her apart inside, brining on a headache and a nauseous stomach. Suddenly feeling vulnerable, she wanted to crawl into her bed under the covers and sleep forever. She wanted to forget Nolan Banks wasn't the man she wished and wanted him to be. She wanted to pretend they'd had a chance. She wanted to pretend he could be her Prince Charming. She wanted to pretend he could be her forever.

"You have to listen to me," he said, hands outstretched in surrender. "I'd never do that. I liked you! I liked talking to you —you were funny and smart. God forgive me, I'm sorry I didn't recognize you, but I would've never made a bet to sleep with you. I don't even remember any of this. I swear to God on everything I hold dear, Presley, you have to believe me."

The fury left, leaving her a dry, empty husk. She shook her head and turned away, needing to retreat. "I can't do this anymore. I can't hear your lies and denial. I can't pretend to be cool and hip, and say I don't care how you hurt me, because I did. But you can't hurt me anymore, Nolan Banks. And I hope you take that to your cold, lonely bed every damn night. Now, leave me the hell alone."

"Presley, no, please—"

She walked out the door without a glance back, knowing this was the only way it could end.

Game over.

CHAPTER 20

HE WAS OFFICIALLY LOSING HIS MIND.

Nolan lifted the mug and took another sip of the stinging, hot brew. He'd been up all night, examining every last shred of memory he had of Presley Cabot, the frat party, and her shocking claims. Wracking his brain, he tried to figure out where he'd gone wrong.

Yes, there were holes that night, but he figured he'd been really drunk. It happened sometimes with his frat brothers. But he never tried to sleep with women when he was drunk, and stayed far away when a female seemed even a bit tipsy. God knows, he learned early on his entire life could be ruined with a claimed date rape or forced encounter, and usually he was the one who kept careful watch on the parties to make sure everyone was safe.

He'd never do something like that. And if he'd slept with Presley, he sure as hell would've remembered it.

Then why was she sticking to her story? Why did she look at him with such raw hurt and fury that it tore him apart?

Some things began to click. He remembered those extraordinary eyes and her smile. Remembered their brief conversation when he mentioned her story from class, and the joy flickering over her face. She was sweet. Funny. He would've talked to her longer, but after that, the rest of the night was blurry.

Nolan groaned with frustration, rubbing his eyes. *Fuck.* Why hadn't he remembered her when she walked into the Bank? Why hadn't her name even jogged his memory?

But she looked so damn different, with her sleek burgundy hair, weight loss, and her cool, sassy attitude. She'd been shy and quiet in writing class, barely speaking. Yes, he was a total asshole for not remembering, but was it worth trying to accuse him of sleeping with her in order to set up an entire humiliation?

Hell no.

It was hard to believe that this entire week had just been an act. A plot for revenge. While he'd been falling hard for her, she'd been faking it and plotting his demise. For the first time in his life, his heart was opening to a woman who hadn't even been interested.

A sharp pain hit his chest but he ignored it. Right now, he had one goal.

Prove her wrong.

It took him a while to find the box of old yearbooks he'd put in the attic storage. He spent time sifting through the one from Boyer University, jogging his memory of the guys he'd hung out with on his track team and who'd been at that party with him that night. He grabbed his laptop and a notepad, and immersed himself into creating a list of contacts to piece the evening back together.

The first few texts and Facebook messages provided nothing but a stroll down memory lane about their all-star days. No one remembered Presley or any type of bet. He shot off a few more emails, making his way down the list, and finally came to Gabe Daniels.

Nolan squinted at his bio, studying his Facebook page. Gabe had been an asshole in the frat house, loud and crude, and constantly riding him on being the untouchable golden boy. Looked like nothing had changed with the stream of posts showing off his new shiny car, his muscles, and his hot model wife. Nolan sure as hell didn't want to reconnect with the guy, but it was important if he remembered anything.

Nolan tapped out a quick message, and left a voice mail on the guy's phone number that was listed online.

He jumped in the shower and tried to wrap his head around Presley's accusations. The idea she'd believe he could do those things made his gut clench. So, she'd been overweight. Big deal. He'd never bullied or judged people—God knows, his sister had been picked on in high school and he'd seen first-hand the way her self-confidence had shattered. Sure, he had a crappy memory, but he'd never had sex with a woman he'd forgotten about. Something told him having Presley naked in his bed, either then or now, would be an experience that stayed with him for a lifetime.

Sick at his revolving thoughts, he got dressed, brewed another pot of coffee, and re-checked his messages.

Gabe had responded.

Hey, man, good to hear from you! Winning any more medals or has your knee finally blown out? Lol. What's up?

Nolan tapped out a response. *Nah, got away from running and into beer. Thanks for getting back to me—had a question about our frat days. Had a party one night after the big Williamsburg College meet—there was a girl with me named Presley Cabot. Remember her?*

Hey, call my cell.

Surprised, Nolan tapped out the number and Gabe picked right up. "Banks, good to hear from you, my brother. Figured it'd be easier to talk."

"Thanks. So, I recently ran into Presley Cabot, and she was trying to tell me about this frat party she went to with us. Do you remember her?"

"Hell, I never cared about names." He laughed. "What'd she look like? Hot?"

Nolan tamped down on his irritation and answered calmly. "Pretty face, gray eyes, blonde hair. Overweight."

"The fat girl! Ah, yeah, of course!" More laugher. "You don't remember banging her, huh?"

Cold dread slithered in his veins. He gripped the phone. "What? I slept with her?"

"Fuck, yeah. Course, we never mentioned it to you. Not surprised you don't remember, dude, you were flying high that night." *Shit, shit, shit.*

His throat tightened and panic began to beat in his chest. "I was drunk? Gabe, tell me everything you know. I never got that drunk before, and it's important."

"Nah, it wasn't just the alcohol. The guys and I slipped a roofie in your drink. You were always such a tight ass and we wanted you to relax and have fun. Saw the fat girl staring at you like you were her next meal, so after you passed out in the bedroom, I sent her into you. Feel free to thank me, but it sucks you don't remember. The shy ones are always the wildest, you know. Hey, where are you living now? I settled in Philly and do some awesome barbeques on the weekend. You're welcome to stop in."

The world spun and he stumbled to the chair, his ass slamming into the seat. His mind tried furiously to grasp onto the most important facts in Gabe's re-telling. "Wait. You drugged me, and then sent Presley into my room? What the fuck did you tell her?"

"Told her you were crazy about her and wanted to see more of her. Ah, fuck, you're not gonna get your panties in a twist just because you finally had some fun, are you?"

"She said something about a bet?"

"Yeah, first we bet you couldn't beat the record on the beer funnel. Then we bet you couldn't fuck the fatty. Course, you were pretty gone by then anyway, so we got you in bed and I figured I'd let you win that bet. Gift wrapped her all up for you, my boy. So, wanna come to Philly? I'm still buds with some of the guys from the frat house, and I bet they'd love to see you."

The reality of what had happened struck him full force. He knew it would be a long time before this conversation wouldn't haunt him, the knowledge he'd been drugged and manipulated to hurt a woman he cared about, the sickness of being used for a cruel, frat joke.

The rage had died into a flat, cold fury that vibrated in his voice. "Listen up, Gabe. You are more than a piece of shit— you're a criminal. You damaged someone's life because of your crap soul, and I swear to God, if I ever see you or hear from you, I'll make you regret that night every day of your life. Got it?" *Fucking hell.*

He clicked off the phone, interrupting the outraged cursing on the other end.

Dragging in a shaky breath, Nolan wrapped his hands around his mug for warmth. It was all true. He'd slept with Presley and remembered nothing. This entire time, she believed he was part of the plot to humiliate her. This entire fake relationship had been about getting even.

God, he couldn't even blame her. He deserved every bit of revenge she tossed his way. And then some.

The real problem was convincing her he had nothing to do with the set up, and he'd also been a victim.

Then he had an even bigger obstacle to overcome.

Trying to show Presley Cabot what they started together was real.

Presley watched Reese Witherspoon dance with the love of her life to the song *Sweet Home Alabama*, then shortly after yell for him to leave her and the past behind.

It all sounded too familiar.

God, she should've put on *Bridesmaids*.

Burying deeper into her cream-colored sofa, she sipped at her champagne and fell into the beauty of her favorite second-chance romance. Certain movies and books allowed her to drift away so she didn't think about her problems, and this was one of her go-tos. Unfortunately, not even her favorite movie distracted her enough from what had happened a few nights ago.

She'd finally wreaked her revenge.

When she called Aubrey and Libby, they'd been happy for the completion of the plan and showed up at her doorstep with champagne. They toasted to getting even. They reminded her Nolan deserved her scorn and were appropriately shocked and outraged at his blatant denial of the truth. Cam sent her a text forgiving her for the black dress incident and proclaimed the end goal had been worth the sacrifice. Trinity left a gloating message of triumph and offered to set her up on a date with a hot journalist she worked with. Everyone had her back and felt like she could finally move onward, the past safely locked behind her in a neat little box.

She wanted them to be right but it felt all wrong. Nolan's face still haunted her—the look of complete confusion and shock when he denied sleeping with her. The Nolan she'd gotten to know didn't seem like a liar or a fraud—only a total gentleman. There was a disjointed piece of the truth that still didn't fit, but the idea of seeing or speaking to him again hurt too much.

She'd decided to take the night for hibernation. Face free of makeup, nerd glasses donned, she'd completed a seaweed facial and stuck her hair up in a clip. Clad in her comfy hot pink heart Lulumons, a faded white t-shirt with the neckline comfortably stretched out, and pink pig slippers that made little oinks when she stepped, Presley intended to watch love movies all night and drink champagne. Eventually, she'd fall asleep or pass out and finally get some peace.

The doorbell rang.

Really? Trinity had threatened to come over but Presley texted her that she craved an alone night. Of course, her friend never listened, and was probably keen on dragging her to some hot club to meet single men to banish the ghost of Nolan Banks.

Like that would help.

Glumly, she padded to the front door and flung open the door. "I told you I don't want to go out—holy shit!"

Nolan stood on her porch, towering in the door with his usual masculine power and grace. Hair mussed, lines bracketing his mouth and eyes, he looked like he hadn't slept in a few days either. His gaze took in her outfit, a glint of amusement briefly dancing in his eyes. "Spa night?" he asked.

She realized her face was full of green mud and she wasn't wearing a bra and stuffed pigs clad her feet.

Oh, no, she refused to be humiliated at this point. She turned and tried to slam the door, but he blocked it with his foot. "You have to go away," she demanded with pure crankiness. "Just forget you ever saw this."

"Presley, I have to talk to you. *Please.* It's important."

The naked plea in his voice made her hesitate. Why was he here? Hadn't they already said everything left between them? Her heart pulsed in her chest with an empty ache she didn't understand. Damn him. Why did he have to keep pushing? She let him in, slammed the door, and turned on her squeaky slippers, jabbing a finger in the air. "Fine, talk. But hurry up because the end of *Sweet Home Alabama* is coming and I refuse to miss it."

"Are you oinking?"

She sneered in his face. "Gonna judge me now, huh? Is my outfit not sexy enough for you? Are you not dazzled enough? Well—too bad, beer man! This is what you get tonight, so either talk fast or get out of my house."

"You were right. We did sleep together."

Her chin dropped. "Really? Now, you're ready to own up to the whole thing, huh? Listen, I'm glad you want to come clean and all, but I'm done. Just leave me alone and go back to your bar."

"No, you don't understand, I was telling the truth. I really had no idea we slept together. I was drugged."

She narrowed her gaze. "I see. I'm supposed to believe our entire sexual encounter was a blur, including the bet you made with your friends?"

He winced. "No . . . Yes. Let me start from the beginning."

He did. He told her the entire conversation with Gabe, what the guy had admitted, and how the evening had played out.

Presley listened. First, she was skeptical, but as he spoke in detail, a flood of doubt washed through her. Everything he said actually made sense. She remembered Gabe's sneer and insult toward Nolan. Would the guy go so far as to drug him? And she knew well about the roofies and how they could banish an entire night of memories.

Had there been truly no bet? No evil plan to humiliate her? Just some rotten frat boys out to play and have some laughs at her expense?

Which would mean Nolan was innocent.

And that was a whole new problem.

Her mind spun with possibilities. She had two paths. Refuse to believe him and throw him out. Or accept his truth and move onward with the understanding too much had happened between them to have any type of relationship—including friendship. Or was there a third path? The one that whispered to her in the background, *'Take a chance on Nolan. Take a chance on love.'*

Not that she wanted to be friends with Nolan. Hell, she could still barely be in his presence without melting like hot caramel, let alone try and play at being his buddy. No, thanks. Better to have a clean break.

"Presley, I know it's a lot to take. Hell, it sounds like a perfect excuse, and I'm not even the one I'm trying to convince. I just want to ask you a question. Is there any possibility you could believe me?"

And that's when she knew. She knew he was telling the truth, from the gleam of righteous indignation mixed with a spark of anger. This was no man on a guilt trip, or trying to lie his way out of a tough situation. And if he was right, that meant he was just as much a victim as she was.

The fight drained out of her body. Once again, her view of the past tilted, and she was forced to view it from a different lens. She squeaked back to the couch and sat down, refilling her champagne glass. Took a sip. And gave him the words he needed. "Yes. I believe you, Nolan."

His breath released like a balloon. He came to sit beside her, keeping a good distance between them. "Thank you. I don't know if we have any recourse at this point with Gabe, but I'll sure as hell pursue it if you want."

She shook her head. "I think we've both had enough of living in the past, don't you?"

His gaze delved deep into hers. "Yes, I do. It's the future we have to discuss."

She cleared her throat, wondering why there was still such a thick sexual tension hanging in the air. It should be gone now. She was back to her old self, yet her body beneath her grungy clothes peaked to attention, and her nostrils danced as his familiar scent swarmed her. The guy was just sex on a stick, and she had to stop craving a lick. If only Nolan weren't so damn desirable. "Want a drink?" she blurted out.

He smiled. "Love one. No, I'll get it." He waved her back to her seat and headed into the open kitchen, grabbing a wine glass from the display. "Can I share your champagne?"

"Of course. You can join me in the celebration."

"You close a big deal?"

Her lips twisted in a half smile. "Nope. Celebrating your wicked demise as the evil villain who seduced me."

He groaned, filled his glass and sat back down. This time, there was only a few inches between them. "That drug must've been potent if it wiped out every memory of you naked in my bed."

Her fingers gripped the flute. A touch of bitterness edged her voice. "I was different back then," she said. "I didn't have sex appeal or confidence, and I was overweight by a good hundred pounds." She winced and took a gulp. The bubbles danced in her throat with mockery. "You wouldn't have remembered it anyway."

His hand shot out and grasped her wrist. Intensity radiated from his aura, and his gaze narrowed with warning. Her heart stuttered out of rhythm as she stared back, fascinated by the male temper flaring his nostrils. "Don't talk about yourself that way," he said, his voice like a whiplash. "It's not fair to either of us. My choice was taken away that night. Who knows what would've happened if Gabe hadn't interfered."

"Don't pretend, Nolan," she fired back. "Everyone knows the fat girl and the golden boy don't work out in the end."

"I'll regret every damn day that your first time was ruined," he said. "That I made you feel unworthy and not the beautiful, sexy woman you are."

She couldn't take it any longer, couldn't pretend to believe the way he spun the past. "I wasn't sexy then, and I'm not sexy

147

now. Oh, sure, I know how to dress and flirt and put on a show. That was actually easy to learn, to try and become the woman you'd fall for. But you know who I really am? The same girl inside I was years ago. The one who tripped and knocked your teeth and ripped my dress. The one who wears pig slippers and cotton to bed. The one who craves reading all the time because I can go away and become someone else for a little while. I changed the outside, and worked damn hard to catch up on the inside, but who knows if I'll ever be there? And this thing we had between us—whatever it was—is over. It was just a mirage. It wasn't real. *We* aren't real, Nolan."

Grasping her upper arms, he reached out and pulled her toward him. She gasped as his mouth hovered inches from hers, her heart suddenly racing a mile a minute. The muscle in his jaw ticked. "Now who's the liar?" he grated out. "Every moment between us was fucking real, sweetheart. This is the woman I really fell for—the one sitting right here beside me. The one who peeked out from her seductress role and made me laugh, and think, and want. You think I'm going to lie and say your body isn't hot? That I don't get crazy when I hear the little hitch in your voice when you're turned on? Or that my dick doesn't get hard as a rock when I look into your eyes and see you want me just as bad?"

His words pummeled her like tiny, stinging rocks, challenging her to hear the truth. "I cop to all of it. But if you think it's just your body and pretty face that's got me tied up in knots, it's time I set you straight. Every conversation we had was real. That kiss we shared was real. Every time you smiled at me and lit up my world was real. You and me together, baby, that's real too. And you're just gonna have to deal with it."

Shaking her head, she tried to pull back, but he refused to allow her retreat.

"I don't know what would've happened between us. I don't know what type of story we would've written together, but we can't go back and figure it out, Presley. The opportunity was taken away from us. But now—we get to choose. No one gets to tell us what we can be together, and I sure as hell don't intend to have another regret by not grabbing my moment. Our moment."

His breath struck her lips, and she stared into ocean blue eyes, caught and held in the glittering emotion found in their depths. "Let's write our own damn love story. Or are you too afraid to try?"

Time stopped. Seconds ticked by, cranking up the swirling, crackling tension and then he muttered a vicious curse and she tilted her head and he was kissing her. She forgot about her green mud mask, her crappy clothes, and bad temper. Presley kissed him back even harder, losing herself in that moment, one where she felt as if he were seeing the real her for the first time.

His tongue invited, seduced, and played. His hands tangled in the crazy mess of her hair, holding her head while she drowned in the kiss, savoring the delicious taste of coffee, mint, and naked male hunger. Slowly, he eased back, nipping at her lower lip, his gaze drilling into hers as his spoken declaration still echoed in the air.

Shuddering, she wrapped her arms around her body, chilled by the loss of his embrace. Her throat tightened with emotion. Despair and vulnerability flooded her. "I think it may be too late," she whispered. "Maybe you're right. Maybe I'm not brave enough to take the risk again. I'm sorry, Nolan."

It was so much better to cut off any hope early on. Because

if she went on this wild ride with him again, this time with her true self, she may not survive another fall-out.

Dropping his hands to his lap in defeat, he studied her face for a long time, probing deep, and then he slowly nodded as he stood up to leave. "I understand."

She tightened her muscles to avoid the ache of the loss, to guard her weeping heart as he moved to the door, even though she knew it was the right move for both of them. His hand paused on the knob.

"Presley?"

Her name danced in her ears, his husky voice a low growl of sound.

"Yes?"

"I'm brave enough for the both of us. This time, I'm not letting you go."

The door closed softly behind him.

His words shattered the last of her fragile defenses. She watched as Reese Witherspoon finally declared her love for the only man in her heart. Clad in her wedding dress, standing in the pouring rain, she said the famous words that claimed her happy ever after.

"Why would you want to marry me for, anyhow?" her hero shouted.

"So I can kiss you anytime I want."

The couple fell into a passionate kiss on the beach.

And Presley burst into tears.

CHAPTER 21

ON WEDNESDAY MORNING, SHE ENTERED STARBUCKS AT EXACTLY 7:58am, skipped the line, and went to the counter. "Hi Mandy," she greeted, automatically reaching for her Grande Skinny Vanilla latte. Her fingers only caught air and she blinked, realizing her coffee wasn't ready. That had only happened once in the past three months due to a glitch in scheduling and the manager had sworn it would never happen again. As one of the few chains in Port Hudson, and necessary for the college crowd, she preferred to give her business to the local coffee shops but this was on her way to LWW and employed a large portion of the town. Besides, she'd been able to help institute more recycling initiatives, including strawless summers that were getting more popular. "Umm, where's my coffee?"

Mandy stuck a finger in the air. "Mr. Banks said he's holding it for you at your table."

Blinking, she tried to clear her vision and maybe her ears, as Nolan wouldn't hold her drink hostage, would he? But no, there he was, perched at the round table in the corner with a smirk shining on his face. He waved his hand back and forth in an attempt to get her attention.

This was not happening.

Her mind quickly rewinded to the night he left. After she'd finished her crying fit, she went to bed and slept for twelve hours straight. When she woke, she'd done her meditation, then threw herself into work, knowing it was the best way to move on. She was in the middle of an auction for a new author she sensed would be a break-out with her first male/male book, and dove into a first-time author's edits, which had been more challenging than usual.

She'd deliberately pushed away Nolan's last words, figuring he'd back off for a while after such an intense scene. By then, she'd be strong enough to keep him out of her life, and they could both move onward.

But he was here. Looking at her with those intense blue eyes. Smirking his grab-her-by-the heart grin. Making the next move after she had basically told him, *'game over.'*

She tamped down a groan. She wasn't looking her best today. She was still a bit raw and grumpy, and hadn't wanted to call Trinity for a fashion therapy session yet, so she'd reached for her old standard black suit, stuck her hair up again, and called it a day.

Even worse? The sight of his lean body sprawled in the too-small chair was seriously drool-worthy. The man caused a pair of jeans to weep with joy, and the casual navy t-shirt made his eyes so blue they almost hurt. He looked fresh and oh-so-sexy, and she wanted to kiss him to see if he tasted like the mocha he was sipping.

Instead, she marched forward, perched her hands on her hips, and glared.

"Why are you holding my coffee hostage?"

He pulled out a chair for her, ushering her to sit. "Trust me, I don't have a death wish. I just wanted to buy your morning coffee and talk. I was afraid you wouldn't take my calls."

"You're right, I wouldn't. This is over, remember?"

He gave a lopsided smile that made her heart flip. "Not for me. How'd you sleep?"

She narrowed her gaze in suspicion. "Why? Are you telling me I look tired?"

His blue eyes danced with humor. "You look amazing. Like a sexy librarian come to life. I like those black glasses you wore the other night."

She coughed, caught off guard. Then sat down. "I have to get to work."

"I know. I called your receptionist who said you usually allow a half hour in the morning to just meditate and drink your coffee to get into your head space for the day."

"Madison told you that?" she squeaked, grabbing her coffee and taking that first hot sip as a lifeline. "She's fired."

"I guess she took pity on me. I told her I was hopelessly infatuated with you and promised I wasn't a crazy, serial stalker."

"Yes, that's helpful. Most serial stalkers know they're crazy and ask for help."

His gaze sharpened with interest. "You're not a morning person, are you?"

She grunted, kept her silence, and sipped.

"You see, this is the stuff that intrigues me. I happen to find myself just as attracted to the woman in the green mask and pig

153

slippers as much as the temptress with the designer dresses. And even though you may fight me, I'm kind of stubborn when I want something. I've always loved a good challenge, and you, book goddess, are the ultimate challenge."

She glared. "Stubborn is just another word for a pain-in-the-ass."

He laughed. "Maybe. How about determined or goal-oriented?"

"Another word for arrogant, and how about changing your goal and game to 'Operation Leave Presley the Hell Alone?"

"Damn, I love it when you're mean. It sparks a fire inside me that only you can put out."

She rolled her eyes, trying not to be charmed. He had this way of casting a spell on her and it couldn't keep going on like this. "What do you really want, Nolan? To win me? To prove I can fall for you? How about we end this little charade right now? I can very easily fall for you again. Okay?"

He beamed. "Okay. So, let's date. You know we've only touched the surface of what we can be together. We need to explore this—explore *us* more."

She blinked. "No, because I know what can happen. I fall for you, you get bored, you break my heart, and we have a do-over of that entire college episode. I want to move on. I don't want to be that scared, insecure girl any longer that I was with you."

A frown furrowed his brow. He leaned over, grasping her hands. "Presley, I don't want you to be that girl either. You're misunderstanding. I want us to date and get to know one another on our terms. To see what's there between us. I want to get real with you."

"I told you—"

"I know what you told me. You're scared. I get it, but I'm

asking for just a few dates. A few dates to get to know each other better. We can still keep our barriers up if you want. We'll take it slow, and see if there's anything we want to keep pursuing. Hell, you may not like me anymore now that you don't want to seduce and dump me. Plus, your friends despise me. That's a big obstacle."

She couldn't help it. A laugh escaped her lips. "I haven't told them what really happened," she admitted. "I needed some time to sort it through myself."

"Oh, good, then there's a chance I can win them over."

She sighed. "Don't know, that's a lot of years of hate built up."

He looked a little despondent before giving her his signature grin while she allowed him to keep holding her hand. "Baby, you underestimate me." His smile turned into an almost forlorn look. "Please, just give me a chance to try. Let me at least take you to lunch before you decide on anything."

She stared at him, studying the earnest lines of his face, the tightened line of his lips. Even though he'd spotted a glimpse of her real self, he wanted to continue. Was she really going to do this? Take the leap and see what they were together? Allow herself to fall for him all over again?

She'd told him no the first time.

But in the harsh morning light, holding his hand in a Starbucks café, a stirring of hope nudged her belly. Just lunch. She could always stop seeing him if she felt it was going in a bad direction. She could finally satisfy some of her curiosity. Maybe they'd both find too much had passed between them and there was no starting over. Maybe they'd end up friends.

Maybe something more.

"Just lunch?" she asked.

His smile was full of sunshine and dazzled her sight. "Just lunch. I can take you to Alberto's any day you're free this week."

The Italian restaurant was upscale, known for homemade pasta, great wine, and an intimate, romantic setting. She pondered the invitation, sipped her coffee, and made a decision.

"Thursday, 11:30am. But not Alberto's, it's too fancy for me. I like to go to Books 'n Crannies during the week and eat at the café."

Surprise flickered across his face. "A billionaire who lunches at a bookshop."

She shrugged. "I told you, I'm not as fancy as my title. I think I may end up boring you."

He laughed then, a big, deep belly laugh that pumped the room full of joy. "Oh, sweetheart, you are so wrong. But only time will prove that to you." He glanced at his watch. "Gotta go, I don't want to throw your schedule off." He got up from the table, pressed a quick kiss to her lips, and winked. "See you, Thursday."

He left the coffee shop. She stared at his retreating back with her head spinning and her mouth open. *What just happened?*

Oh, yeah.

She was going to have to tell the gang about this very soon.

CHAPTER 22

"Hɪ."

"Hi."

Nolan fought the urge to wipe his palms down his jeans like a nervous teen. Is this what he'd been missing out on all this time? The excitement stirring in his gut? The anticipation zinging his nerves? The clawing hunger to touch, taste, and claim a woman?

She stood in the doorway of LWW headquarters, a tentative smile on her face. As usual, she was dressed to bring a man to his knees, from the sleek red sheath dress that skimmed her lush curves, teetering heels, to the slightly tousled burgundy hair that caught the light and shimmered like a temptress halo. Her lips were pouty red. Her perfume was sweet citrus and exotic spice.

But something had shifted between them. A softness shimmering in the air, sizzling with connection and possibilities. He couldn't help the dopey grin from overtaking his face while he just stood and stared at her.

His brother would have a field day with this.

"I told you I'd meet you there," she said.

"Not on a date. Unless this is your way of hiding me from your friends and co-workers?"

He appreciated her honesty when she met his gaze. "Actually, I just wanted to keep it between us for a few days. Enough to get my footing."

It stung, but he liked her directness. "I get it. I'll just have to work harder to get you to shout my name to the rooftops." He gave her a wink. "Or shout it in other ways."

He caught the red on her cheeks and laughed, casually linking his fingers with hers as they walked. The sunshine was bright, the sky was blue, and the path was paved, leading from LWW Enterprises straight into Main Street.

"How is your day going?"

She wrinkled her nose. "Frustrating. I lost an important auction on a book I wanted, dealt with a prima donna celebrity who believes her tell-all deserves an extra million in advances, and had to yell at one of my friends who's late on deadline."

"Is it worth the extra million?"

"Hell, no. She's a housewife. There's only so much you can tell."

"Will your friend forgive you?"

"Yes, because she'll get the second part of her advance and be able to pay her bills."

He laughed, swinging her arm back and forth in an easy rhythm. The click of her heels on the pavement mixed with the chatter of birds and humans as they reached the center of town. "You're sexy when you're angry and feisty," he said.

"You are one strange man. How was your day?"

"Good. Opening day is coming up and the soft launch showed me the holes I need to plug to make things smoother, especially in the kitchen. I'll be working on a few new batches of beer the rest of the week. Oh, I also looked into that recycling company you mentioned. They're coming to do an analysis and see where we can economize and incorporate some better environmental techniques."

She tilted her head to stare up at him. "You really called them?"

"Yes."

"I thought you were just pretending to be interested in that stuff to get me into bed."

He didn't miss a beat. "I intend to get you into bed, but I'm also interested in the recycling." He caught her when she stumbled slightly and shot her a grin. "We're here."

They entered the Books 'n Crannies Bookshop. There were two main bookstores in town, but the college students preferred the one near Boyer University that combined academic texts so it was one-stop shopping. But Books 'n Crannies was for the serious buyer. They even had a rare book section in a separate room, and there were no silly games, stuffed animals, or gadgets to distract from the main product.

Books. All about the books.

He watched Presley take a deep sniff and close her eyes in pleasure. Her entire being seemed to come alive in the world she loved and with which she had made a successful career. "Doesn't it smell so good?" she murmured.

For a moment, he forgot they were taking it slow and almost pulled her into his arms to kiss her, to be wrapped up in the joy and enthusiasm of her moment. But then she was spinning around and tugging him down the aisle. "Let's play a game."

He smiled. "I love games. Bring it."

"We each pick out a book for the other and agree to read it."

"Is it to torture the other? Or to be happy?"

She laughed. "No, to be happy. I think we've done enough torturing between us, don't you?"

He couldn't help but reach out and touch her hair. "Yeah, I do. How long do we have?"

"Ten minutes. Meet you at the cashier, then we'll have lunch."

"Deal." He turned to head to the right but her voice stopped him. "Yeah?"

"It can't be a sex book."

He paused. "For me or you?"

"Either."

"Damn. Okay, I'm gonna need more time." His idea of implementing the latest Kama Sutra book evaporated. Time to stop thinking sexy thoughts and focus on non-sex books.

She shot him a look, then disappeared around the corner. He took some time to browse, his mind skittering through various possibilities. She was a voracious reader. Eclectic. Probably hard to surprise. But this was also personal, his first gift to her after the flowers. It had to be something that fit.

And then he was standing next to it.

He pulled out the leather book, beautifully bound with tinted dark green edged pages, and a satin bookmark. His hand stroked the cover and then he brought it up to the counter.

She was already there waiting for him, her purchase bagged.

"Don't look," he warned, hiding the book behind his back. "We'll reveal at lunch."

He completed the purchase and they headed toward the back, taking a seat in two mismatched velvet chairs. "What do you like here?" he asked, settling himself in the deep cushions.

"The cranberry turkey club."

"Done." Darlene came over, took their orders, and dropped off two seltzers. "You're right. This is much better than a fancy carb-laden lunch. What other places do you like to haunt?"

She propped her elbows on the small table. "Quarters."

"Ouch. Hopefully you'll upgrade."

She smiled. "Is it strange being back? I remember when we built LWW here, I'd changed so much but the town hadn't. Oh, sure, there were some new stores and a batch of new students, but the actual core of Port Hudson was exactly the same."

"Still must've been nice to come in like a conquering hero." He paused, wondering how much to push. "It sounded like college was hard here for you. Is that why you wanted to come back? To prove a point?"

A sigh spilled from her lips. Her face became thoughtful. "To be honest, other than my weight, I loved college. I found my best friends, and started our own sorority, which was more of a sisterhood than a formal club. I studied writing. I became who I was meant to be. And it was those same friends who helped me lose the weight, so I'd look as good on the outside as I felt inside."

"Was there a particular reason you struggled with your weight?"

"It was strange. My parents loved and supported me. They cooked healthy, and it wasn't like they were huge junk eaters. But I remember, even while young, I was always hungry. I always thought about food. Hell, I obsessed over food and how much I'd get at meals, and how to finagle extra desserts. I craved more. Mom took me to the doctor as I kept packing on the weight. I dealt with crazy diets I cheated on, and exercise routines that only humiliated me. Finally, it became this emotional see-saw that overtook my life. High school was hard, but I worked at the library and a bookstore, and made some friends. But by then, it wasn't about losing twenty pounds anymore. It was overwhelming, and easier just to keep eating."

His heart hurt thinking of how she'd struggled. Adolescence was like being dropped into a shark tank and told to swim to safety. A percentage never seemed to make it out. "I can't imagine how hard that must've been for you."

"Yeah, it kind of sucked. But I graduated college and a bunch of my friends decided to be my core crew and help me lose the weight. It was like having help twenty-four seven and I didn't have to pay a dime." She grinned. "Aubrey and Libby were my gym partners, and Trinity helped me with my wardrobe and kept it real about how I was feeling. I was kind of her trial run for her career as a fashion therapist. I learned to reach for healthy snacks rather than fast food and sugar. It was a slow process, sometimes painful and always frustrating, but eventually, it taught me the two most important lessons in life."

"What's that?"

"Anything is possible if you want it bad enough and work hard enough. Kind of a good deal, huh?"

He leaned forward, completely captivated. "What's the second lesson?"

"Everyone is beautiful," she said simply. "You just need to believe it yourself."

He was overtaken by her honesty, by the simple way she expressed her soul to him. That moment, sitting in the café, he finished his fall completely.

He fell in love with Presley Cabot.

Ridiculous. They had a messy past. They'd started their relationship on a lie. They'd had only one official real date.

Yet, there it was. The truth came up from inside him, and Nolan accepted it. All his life, things had come easy, causing him to worry if the gift would strip him of the opportunity to cherish. He realized he no longer had that worry. He'd fought hard to finally leave Wall Street and run his own bar. That hadn't been easy, and he loved every inch of the place he could finally call his.

With Presley, it was easy to love her. The problem was breaking down all of her walls to allow her to fall in love with him. It wouldn't be easy, but if he gained her heart, he knew he'd treasure it forever. He'd never take her for granted.

Now, he had to hope she was on the same path.

And instead of harps, heartfelt declarations, and romance in that sacred moment, Darlene plopped their turkey clubs in front of them, and Presley dug in, without a thought to the monumental realization he'd just experienced.

Nolan began to laugh.

She tilted her head and studied him with curiosity. "What's so funny?"

"I'll tell you one day."

Then he bit into his sandwich.

This date was going way too well.

Presley watched him enjoy his lunch and wondered why being with him felt so natural and right. She'd expected after what they've been through—after all the lies, revelations and emotion, they'd be awkward with each other. She'd figured by the end of lunch, they'd agree to go their separate ways.

Instead, she'd dumped her entire life story and hidden secrets in the first afternoon.

She was so uncool.

He'd looked a little loopy after her confession. Probably wondering why he'd agree to pursue the crazy girl with the seaweed masks, chick flicks, and piggy slippers. But it was too late to pull back now. Might as well eat her sandwich and wait 'til he politely dumped her again after he picked up the bill. Actually, it wouldn't be considering dumping her since they never agreed to a relationship, right? It just would be a decision for him to not call her again.

"I'm wondering if you'd tell me about that night we slept together."

She dropped her turkey back on the plate and stared at him. "Huh?"

He seemed calm, popping a kettle baked chip in his mouth. "The night we slept together. Since I don't remember a damn thing, you have the advantage over me. Will you tell me about it? Unless it makes you uncomfortable?"

"Umm, no. I mean, sure. I mean, well, it was a very long time ago and I try not to think of that night."

"I understand. But was I—" he cut himself off, looking down at his plate. His brow furrowed. "Was I rough? Did I hurt you?"

"No." She reached out and gripped his wrist. His gaze swiveled back to hers and she was trapped by the deep ocean blue of his eyes, and the flare of worry there. "Nolan, listen to me. You were gentle. To be honest, I was the one who pursued you." She gave a half laugh. "I literally climbed into bed, naked, and asked for you to . . . umm . . . have sex with me. It wasn't like you ever took advantage. Okay?"

He swallowed. Pure relief carved out the lines of his face. "Thank God. It's been bothering me if I did something to make the whole thing worse."

"You didn't. I swear."

"Good." He popped another chip, chewed, then regarded her thoughtfully. "Did you have an orgasm?"

This time, she choked on the bite, and ended up sucking down the rest of her seltzer. "What?"

"Orgasm. You know. Did I at least give you that?"

A redness formed on her face as heat surged through her at the memory of her telling all her friends he was a sucky lay. She fiddled with the napkin in her lap. "Oh. Well, no."

"Probably because it was your first time. Still, there's no excuse." She felt his gaze probe her face, but kept her gaze downward. His next question was laced with suspicion. "Presley, was the sex good?"

Oh, God.

"Sure," she lied.

"Look at me."

The demand cut through the air. She gulped in a breath and raised her gaze.

"Was the sex good for you, Presley?"

She sighed. "No. It wasn't good."

He groaned and rubbed his forehead. "Ah, *shit.*"

She patted his arm in reassurance. "It's okay, Nolan. You were roofied. You tried."

He made another painful noise and shook his head. "This could be one of my lowest moments, and I've had a few."

"Don't worry about it. I really liked the cuddling. Oh, and the kiss. That was awesome."

"Oh, God, it's getting worse. When you like the cuddling better than the sex, a man should be locked up and jailed, and maybe retire his balls."

She went back to eating. "You're being so dramatic. Not every man is great in bed. Most women like the emotional bond of sex even better than the actual orgasm, you know. Remember, it's all mental."

He lifted his head and gave her such a sizzling stare that her body froze and then burst to life. Those blue eyes glittered with intensity. "Presley, I'm very good at sex. Trust me when I say I know how to satisfy a woman."

She blinked. Her stomach did a flip-flop and dipped to her toes. "I believe you."

That delicious mouth firmed into a thin line. "No, you don't. I'll have to prove it to you."

This time, her panties dampened and her thighs squeezed together. Dayum, that was hot. Who would've thought a man declaring himself good at sex could turn her on? Or maybe it was the hungry way he stared at her like he was the predator and she was his prey, like he was just seconds from laying her out on the table and giving her all sorts of dirty pleasures. The thought of their hot kiss on the grass stirred her memory. She had absolutely no doubt Nolan Banks was a pure God in the sack, and she can't wait to test his skills and let him pleasure her in every way.

But she didn't have to let him know that just yet.

She shrugged. "Sure. One day, maybe. For now, let's just finish up our lunch. It's time to exchange our gifts."

He kept staring at her with that determined look. "I'm owed a re-do."

"A what?"

"A re-do. A repeat of us in bed, so I can show you the right way. It's only fair that you let me pleasure you, Presley."

She rolled her eyes after first thinking how hot his words sounded and what a tempting offer he presented, one she did not have to ponder. "Sure, *you're* owed a re-do. That's convenient. What if I said, no thanks? Been there, done that, wrote the book."

He winced. "Dear God, I hope you didn't write a book on that. Or tell all your friends I was a lousy lay. Holy shit, you did tell them, didn't you? Of course, you did. Now, you really owe me."

Why did he have to be so sexy and adorable? She wanted to run her finger over that plump lower lip, smooth out the crease in his brow, trace the marks of his scar. Instead, she fisted her hands under the table and hung on. "I think technically it should be called a do-over. But we're not having a do-over or a re-do just so you can salvage your ego."

"Do you think three orgasms would make up for it? Or four? Be honest."

She swayed in the chair, a bit woozy as all the blood rushed from her head and dropped between her legs. "And we are definitely not talking about orgasms at our first lunch date."

"Fine. Four, it is. And I promise you, sweetheart, when I'm done with you, you'll forget that night ever existed."

Her skin prickled. Sexual chemistry crackled in the air around them. Still, she wasn't about to let him win that easily. The man needed to sweat it out a bit. After all, it truly hadn't been good sex. She shot him a reassuring smile. "Of course, Nolan, I'm sure I will. Now, can I have my present?"

Frustration simmered around him, but he grabbed his package and slid it over to her. Tingling with anticipation, she pulled out the book from the crinkly paper and gazed at the book.

Leaves of Grass by Walt Whitman.

"Poetry?" she whispered. Her hand stroked the cover, carefully bending it back to expose the pages. "You bought me poetry?"

"I'm not sure if you like it, but Whitman is my favorite poet. Have you read his work?"

She shook her head. "No, my electives didn't include a poetry class. I studied some poets but we never went over Whitman."

"I think you'll enjoy him." His voice dropped and rumbled with a dark, velvety richness that sent shivers down her spine. "Sensuality drips from the pages. The words are rich and thick, like honey on the tongue when you speak them aloud. He's a very earthy poet, using the senses to bring out not only an emotional connection, but a physical one too. Especially *I Sing the Body Electric*."

Her body stilled, caught up in his own spell of words he wove around her. Her surroundings dropped away and it was as if they were here alone, in a crowded café, caught in a bubble. The words got stuck in her throat. "Thank you."

His eyes burned hot and bright. "You're welcome."

Her hands trembled when she handed over his own package. She watched his face as he slid it from the bag, studying the cover for a while before he lifted his head. "The Bathroom Reader Updated Edition?"

"I figured you hadn't gotten the newest installment yet."

She held her breath and waited. After such a touching gesture of Whitman, she wasn't sure what he'd think of her own pick for him.

And then, Nolan Banks laughed. Throwing back his head, he laughed long and hard, deep and loud, and at that very moment, Presley realized she was in love with him.

Ah, hell.

Bastard.

CHAPTER 23

SWEAT POURED OFF HER IN WAVES. NAUSEA PITCHED HER stomach. Her lungs burned as she tried to gulp in more air. If she did one more step, she'd die. She was too young to go out like this. Had to rest. Had to—

"You slowing down on me, Cabot?" the drill sergeant voice boomed out near her left ear. "What happened this week? You have a pity party with too much ice cream and wine?"

Well, yes, actually she did.

Presley gasped, bearing down mentally to push harder as she ran her ass on the treadmill with the incline at death level. She didn't bother to answer, knowing she may hurl if she tried to form words, so she just stripped herself down to the basic level and kept running.

The small cry of distress to her right was Aubrey, who may or not be crying.

Libby, on the other hand, still had a zen smile on her face and glowed, rather than sweat.

Bitch.

"Better. Let's start the countdown, five more minutes. Go."

Presley ran and prayed for death, then prayed for survival as the last five minutes of her workout ticked by as slowly as a sloth crosses the road.

"Time. Nice work, ladies. Cool it down."

Presley slowed the pace, her trembling legs barely supporting her. Trinity tossed her a towel, her face wreathed in a satisfied smile. After her legs began to steady, she gulped down her bottle of water, wiped her face, and glared at her friend. "Just for the record, you're fired. You are the worst personal trainer in history. You suck."

Trinity stuck out her tongue and strolled to the mirror to preen. In her vivid black and pink zebra leggings, tight tank top, and elaborate braids twisted on top of her head, she looked in top athletic and fashion form. "You can't fire me 'cause I'm not a trainer and I don't get paid. I do it to keep you healthy. As a favor."

"You like it!" Aubrey accused, finally able to get her voice back. She fell off the treadmill and collapsed on one of the mats. "You look happy when we're suffering!"

Trinity shrugged. "So, what? You're the ones who built an entire gym at headquarters so you'd keep everyone fit. Hell, you even give them half an hour of free time to work out. You have a responsibility as the owners to follow your own advice."

"You are evil," Presley whispered, shaking her head.

Libby jumped off the treadmill and clucked her tongue. She radiated energy. "Guys, you're being really ungrateful here. Trin takes time away from her own schedule to make sure we get our regular workouts in."

Trinity sniffed. "Finally, a voice of reason. Thank you, Libby."

"Welcome. Now, I better get showered and changed. I have to meet with the Make a Wish Foundation who's looking to partner up with us at the annual 5K run through the park."

Aubrey groaned, finally rolling to her feet. "Yeah, I have to yell at some people who are late on a television script."

"Cam and I are meeting up tonight for dinner. Anyone want in?" Trinity asked.

Everyone chimed in a yes. Presley remained silent, engaged in drinking her water.

All gazes turned. "Pres? What's been going on with you? You've ghosted us a few nights this week," Trinity said.

Ah, crap. It was a miracle they hadn't found out that she and Nolan were officially dating. After bribing Madison not to tell anyone about the Starbucks incident, they'd managed to avoid small town gossip for the past few days, but their luck was running out.

"Well, there is something I wanted to say." She cleared her throat. "Umm, remember when I told you about how I'd rather rip off a band aid than peel it off in slow inches?"

Trinity nodded. Libby and Aubrey looked confused.

"Good. Well, Nolan and I are now dating. Can't make it tonight cause we're having dinner. Gotta run. I have to see an author within the hour. See ya."

She bounded to her feet and almost reached the door.

Almost.

Trinity and Aubrey each grabbed a shoulder and forcibly turned her around. Damn, they were quick.

"You're what?" Aubrey screeched. "Oh my God! He did it

again! Put a spell on you like a vampire! I should've loaded you up with garlic."

Trinity shook her head. "She needs an intervention. I heard about this cool thing called break-up camp. People who can't get over another person go there and spend a week grieving and healing over the relationship. It's gotten amazing reviews. I can get you in, Pres."

"Guys, it's okay. It's under control. Will you at least hear me out?"

Libby waved her hand in the air, shushing her friends as they began yelling over each other. "Let Presley talk, please. This is important."

Everyone quieted down.

"I haven't told you the real story about Nolan Banks."

She detailed everything about that night, explaining what had happened, and leading up to his declaration on her couch, the morning coffee date, and their lunch. They'd met a few more times for late night dinners, strengthening the bond even more. Finally, she fell into silence, awaiting their opinion.

Aubrey was the first to speak. "Madison is in huge trouble for keeping this from me."

"She had no choice. I blackmailed her. Told her if she didn't keep my secret, I'd tell Tony in accounting that she was secretly in love with him but was too shy to admit it."

Libby winced. "That's mean. Tony's an asshole."

"I know, I had no choice. Guys, I'm taking this slow. Real slow. I just feel like I may owe it to myself to explore. He's not the person we thought he was."

"He was taken advantage of too, that night," Libby said quietly. "Drugging him? Setting you up? It's a crime. Breaks my heart you both had to go through this."

"Do you trust him enough?" Aubrey asked. "Because you've been secretly in love with him since you were nineteen. And if he hurts you again, I swear to God, I will hire Jack to kill him."

Trinity nodded. "And I'll let her."

Presley groaned and rubbed her temples. "I don't know! I just know he lights me up from inside and I feel so alive around him. I like talking to him. He makes me laugh and feel good about myself. But then, but then . . ."

"Then what?" Libby asked.

"Then I wreck it by wondering again if he could really like me. The real me—not the image I put on to seduce him and wreak my revenge."

"But he said he did," Libby pointed out. "And that he wanted to get to know that part of you."

Her lower lip trembled. "What if it's not enough?"

"Oh, God, you're in love with him again, aren't you?" Aubrey asked.

She nodded miserably. "Yeah. I am."

In seconds, her friends surrounded her in warmth and comfort. "If you're not enough for him, then he wasn't meant for you," Aubrey said simply.

"And you're strong enough to handle it," Trinity added.

"But you have to believe it deep inside," Libby said. "Do you? Because if you love him, you have to take a risk. You have to risk your heart. It's the only way you'll really know if it can work."

Did she? Yes, there were still insecurities. Yes, there was still doubt like when she felt ill at ease in her own body, clumsy, and silly. But didn't most people feel like that on the inside? It was about pushing through and trying to be her best self. That's how she'd lost the one hundred pounds. The motivation hadn't been to be a sexy, glamour girl who brought men to their knees.

The motivation had been to be her best, healthy, wonderful, bad ass self.

On her terms. Just like she'd told Nolan at the bookstore.

The reminder took hold and, slowly, she found her balance again with her friends right by her side.

"I forgot," she said, fighting back the sheen of tears. "Thanks for the reminder, guys."

"We got your back, girlfriend," Trinity said. "Do you want me to dress you for your dinner date tonight? Hot, classy, and bad-assy?"

"Yes, please."

"Are you gonna have sex?" Aubrey asked.

She gulped in a breath. "Hell, I hope so."

"Good. I know exactly what you need to wear to feel strong and to own who you are. An outfit to remind you," Trinity said.

Aubrey and Libby smiled. "That sounds perfect," they said in unison.

Presley took a deep breath and decided to re-set. It was time to take a leap with her feelings.

It was time for a do-over and hopefully a do-*her*-over.

CHAPTER 24

WHEN NOLAN PICKED HER UP FOR DINNER, HE WONDERED IF HE'D be able to get through the evening without ravishing every part of her.

Out of all the outfits she'd worn, this one was the sexiest. Her jeans were well worn, holes in the knee, and cupped her hourglass figure like a lover, emphasizing every mouthwatering, ripe curve. Her t-shirt was black, with sequins stitched over the front that declared *LWW Badass*. Her belt had sparkly jewels embedded in it. Her flip flops were simple black leather. Her hair was pinned up.

And those smoky gray eyes met his through her thick-rimmed, black glasses.

She was magnificent.

"I hope we're not going somewhere fancy schmancy," she quipped, floating out of her home with queenly demand. "I'm not dressed for such an occasion."

"Sweetheart, right now I could take you to the royal ball and be the envy of every man."

Her face softened and he caught a glint of longing in her eyes. He hoped like hell she was getting as caught up with him as he was with her. A one-sided love affair sucked. "Thanks."

He escorted her into the car. "I'm taking you back to my place. I'm cooking."

He got in the driver's seat and pulled out. "I didn't know you could cook," she said.

"My parents were always too busy with work, so we had a private chef. She was amazing and taught my brother and me how to prepare a mean meal."

"What about your sister?"

He scoffed. "Landon? Hell, no. She gets allergic the moment she gets around a pot or pan."

She tossed him a dazzling smile. "I'd like to meet her. She sounds like my kind of person."

"The two of you could rule the world. I'll keep you apart, thank you very much."

He enjoyed her easy laugh and finished the short drive to The Bank, pulling up beside his home. When they walked in, the scents of garlic and spice hit his nostrils. He led her into the kitchen and plucked two wine glasses from the cupboard. "Red or white?"

"White, please."

She slid onto one of the high stools by the Tuscan granite countertop and took in his domain. "You really can cook. Are those copper pots?"

"Of course."

"An espresso machine? Juicer? And what's that?"

"Jumbo food processor."

She blinked. "But you're only one person. Who else do you cook for?"

He shrugged. "Just me. But I like big gadgets and I cannot lie."

She laughed and he poured them both a glass of Chardonnay. He uncuffed and rolled up his sleeves before donning a plain white apron. Turning toward the device, he gave the command. "Alexa, play my cooking list."

The sounds of Imagine Dragons beat over the speakers and he winked. "Now, we're ready."

"What are we having?"

"Pecan-encrusted salmon, spinach, and wild grain rice. Sound good?"

"Sounds like heaven. I could get spoiled."

"I could get used to spoiling you," he said simply.

Her cheeks flushed. Suddenly, the air around them charged and whipped up like a burst of flames. He was getting used to the way she made his body tighten and ache, the need to step close and connect. He heard her tiny gasp, and, suddenly, the easy camaraderie exploded into something much more.

"Don't say things like that unless you mean it," she finally said in a slightly strangled voice.

He approached the counter. Propped his elbows on the counter, he leaned in as he looked at her intently. "What makes you think I don't mean it?"

"It's too soon."

"No, it's not."

She straightened up in her seat and shot him a glare. Her glasses bumped down her nose a few notches. Her eyes darkened to storm gray. God, he adored this woman's fiery strength, underneath a sweet, generous heart. Her prim tone contradicted the naked hunger on her face. "I hope this whole cooking thing isn't a ploy to get me into bed."

He watched her pupils dilate and her pulse pound and realized she wanted him. But she was going to make him work for it, which made her his perfect match. She understood. Knew his tendency to allow things to fall neatly into his lap, and she refused to let him be lazy if he wanted to claim her. His blood roared with anticipation and his dick hardened.

"I don't need a ploy, sweetheart. I bet if I touched you just once, I'd get my do-over."

She sniffed haughtily. "I highly doubt it. Good looks and mediocre charm may seduce some women, but not me."

"Oh yeah?" He cocked his head, his gaze on her pursed apple-red lips. "You think I'm good looking?"

She rolled her eyes. "Duh. Wait—did you just give me the smolder look?"

"Why? Is it not working? I've been perfecting it just for tonight."

Her lips twitched. "It's good, but I told you before. A woman's biggest sexual organ is her brain."

Her intoxicating, all-woman scent teased his nostrils. He was so damn turned on, the blood roared in his head. But he wasn't about to lose this round. It was the most important challenge of his life so far, and he was after the big prize.

Not just Presley Cabot's body.

Her heart.

He got himself back under control and gave her a slow smile. "Good to know. I'll work on it."

He turned back to the stove, and began chatting about the

brewery, smug that he'd spotted the sharp gleam of disappointment in her eyes at his retreat.

Game on, baby.

∽

He was driving her mad.

Presley finished the rest of her meal, her taste buds still singing from the perfectly cooked salmon. She figured her challenge would be enough to rile him up. Why hadn't he tossed her on the counter and tried to ravish her? She'd been ready. She still was ready. After all, she'd prepped for tonight. Donned sexy underwear under her jeans. Wore a lacy, cleavage-flattering bra. Gotten a bikini wax.

She'd practically drooled when she caught him in action as chef. Shirt sleeves rolled up to bare tanned, sinewy arms. Collar open as if he'd just ripped off a tie. Jeans that held a European flare, cutting close to his body to cup his tight ass and hard thighs. He moved in the kitchen with a masculine grace that held her spellbound. His oaky colored hair fell in tousled waves over his brow. A slight shadow hugged his jaw, emphasizing the strong cut and angular features of his face. He was beauty in motion—the true golden boy—and she wanted him more than she ever had anyone else in her life.

Instead, he'd backed off and actually finished dinner. For the past hour, he'd kept the conversation light, making her laugh, and pretending to ignore the ratcheting sexual tension between them that grew stronger every second.

How much could the man really take?

She drained her second glass of wine and studied him. "Dinner was wonderful," she said. "I'm impressed."

"It's not over yet." His words sang with promise. Her tummy clenched. "There's apple cobbler for dessert."

She glared. Now, she was just getting pissed off. It was time to get things moving. "How lovely. So, you said you'd be up to the task of four orgasms. Personally, I think you shot high. But maybe you learned more finesse? I mean, even a vibrator never got me to four. I just don't want you to set yourself up for failure the second time around, you know?" Take that. He wanted to play games? It was time to meet her challenge.

The air grew heavy and still, like the dangerous quiet of a sunny day before the violent hurricane hit. He'd gone completely motionless, his fingers clenched around his wine glass. Slowly, he set it down on the table and swiveled his heated gaze to meet hers.

Presley sucked in a breath at the ferocious hunger glinting in his eyes. The veneer of civility ripped away, and there was only a primitive male before her, a predator paused to strike.

"You challenging me, sweetheart?" he asked softly.

She swallowed. Tried to speak, failed, then tried again. "Umm, no. Yes. Whatever."

He got up from his chair and stalked her like a lion who'd just spotted his prey. Pinned to her seat, frozen in fascination, she waited for him, her heart rapping loudly enough to compete with the music still playing in the background. With one quick motion, he spun the chair around, braced his palms on both arms, and leaned in.

"You're a publications billionaire and you used the word *whatever*."

She licked her lips. She wanted to lick him. Up close, his eyes glittered like sapphire diamonds. His scent wrapped around her, a mix of cotton and sunshine and everything clean and beautiful. His lower lip was a touch fuller than his upper one. The cleft in his jaw was pronounced when he got riled up.

"Whatever."

His lower lip quirked. His gaze raked over her, as if deciding how far he was going to take it. Presley hoped that her sassy mouth would take it far.

Very, very far.

"I won't accept that word, Presley. Right now, I intend to give you what I promised and what you deserve." With easy motions, he unclipped her hair and removed her glasses, putting them on the table. Then pressed forward. His breath struck her mouth and a tiny moan vibrated out of her chest. She was wet between her thighs. Her nipples tingled and itched for his fingers. "A re-do."

She dug deep and found one last rally. "Thought a re-do was for you," she said, trying to sneer. "For your ego."

A devastating smile curved his lips. "No, sweetheart. It's never been about my ego. It's about giving you so much pleasure that you beg me to stop. It's about satisfying you so completely, in all ways. Because you deserve it all. And I won't stop until you do beg—loudly and often—so let's get started, shall we?"

His mouth took hers.

She was lost.

She never wanted to be found.

His warm, firm mouth moved over her lips and his tongue dove inside, devouring her like a starving man, devouring her whole. She moaned and slid her fingers into his hair, hanging on as he ravished, bending her back so she had to give him everything.

And he took it all. His lips on her neck, his breath in her ear, his teeth nipping the sensitive curve of her shoulder. She arched up, pressing her body against his, and he muttered a curse and picked her up from the chair to march into his bedroom. She registered a quick view of masculine comfort—a massive bed with a dark wood headboard, navy blue and crisp white, oak floors. Then her back was cushioned by pillows, and he was stripping off her belt and jeans, leaving her bottom half naked except for the scrap of expensive red lace panties she'd purchased just for the occasion. Just for him. All for him.

He sat back on his heels, his legs bracketing her thighs, his gaze hungrily roving over like he was about to feast. She waited for the shyness to hit, the usual awkwardness of the first naked encounter, but there was nothing but urgency and a burning emptiness she needed to fill.

"You're so fucking beautiful."

She blinked. The raw truth of his words hit her in all the broken places and mended them. "So are you." She tugged at his shirt buttons but he shook his head, gently pulling her hands away and pressing them into the mattress. "What are you doing?"

"Slowing things down."

She frowned, shifting her weight to move closer. "I like fast."

"Seems like we did fast the first time. Now we do slow. I want to take my time with you, Presley. I want to savor every inch of you, as I pleasure you, again and again."

Before she could reply, his delicious, talented mouth, kissed her while his hands roved everywhere on her naked skin. Yanking up her shirt, he unclasped her bra and palmed her breasts while she murmured his name. His thumbs tweaked the hard tips of her nipples, a little rough, a little mean, and then he broke from her mouth to soothe and tongue the burning tips,

183

sucking gently until she ground her pussy madly against the hard length of his thigh, crazed for friction.

He caressed her belly, moved lower, and dove underneath the elastic to touch her.

Her body tightened with anticipation, every muscle locked and loaded as he brushed her clit, curling his fingers as he dove deep inside her channel with one perfect thrust.

She came. Hard.

The orgasm shattered through her, and she cried out, her legs shaking as the delicious sensations ripped along her nerve endings in waves.

"So beautiful," he murmured, his fingers still buried in her pussy. "But we need to go slower."

She groaned, tossing her head, but she caught his wicked grin and then he was lowering himself between her thighs, pushing her wide apart, and his tongue replaced his fingers.

Heaven and hell. Demon and angel. Jailer and liberator.

His thumbs held her open while he licked her slowly and thoroughly, teasing strokes that gave her none of the pressure she needed and all of the shivery thrills to keep her right at the edge of a sensual explosion. His teeth nibbled her throbbing clit, and he licked the sides, gently closing his lips around to suck.

She dug her heels into the mattress and chanted his name in broken cries.

She begged.

Finally, those talented fingers twisted again inside, and he ran his tongue over the top with firm precision.

She came again. Even harder.

"You're so sweet. Taste so good," he whispered, pressing his cheek against her thigh. He moved up, smoothing back her damp hair, kissing her again so she tasted herself on his lips. "I could devour you forever."

"Off. Clothes," she said drunkenly, desperately pulling at his shirt. "Need to touch you."

He got up, divesting himself of his clothes, and stood before her in his naked glory. Her gaze roved over the muscled breadth of his chest, his chiseled abs, his sinewy arms, and his hard and rather large dick. He stood erect like a statue of a Greek god. Hips braced apart, head proudly up, he let her drink in her fill before laying a packet on the side table and getting back on the bed.

His male beauty was stunning, but she couldn't speak, could only touch him everywhere. Her fingers, nails, and palms were mad for the feel of his hot skin. His crisp hair tickled as their limbs tangled together, and she licked him, loving the salty spice against her tongue, swallowing his moans with her own lips when she finally dragged his mouth back to hers.

She barely heard the rip of the condom. He pushed her knees up and out, spreading her wide, and pressed inside her with slow deliberate movements that drove her half mad, until she dug her nails into his hips and surged upward for more.

He gritted his teeth and cursed. Sweat popped over his brow. "Sweetheart, you're killing me. I said *slow*."

"And I said *fast*. I need you, Nolan. I need you."

His gaze drilled into hers and she let him see it all, the river of raw emotion chopping through her, and then with a shout, he buried himself to the hilt and claimed her. She clung to him as he began to move, her body clenching tight around him, refusing to let him go, and he thrust deeper, harder, and faster, pressing her deep into the mattress.

The next orgasm burst through her and bloomed heat into

every inch of her body. She gave herself up to the excruciating pleasure, panting, her body boneless.

"Presley."

She stared into ocean blue eyes that held everything she ever wanted. "Again. I want to memorize your face when I make you mine."

His lips covered hers. He sipped, nipped, and played while he built her back up slowly, his throbbing dick filling her, giving her clit the perfect friction, until she hung on the edge again.

This time, she fell apart while she looked into his eyes.

This time, he was right with her for every step.

And this time, when it was over, he held her tight and whispered her name and kept her safe.

In the dark. Pressed against his hard chest. His hands in her hair. Her leg tangled between his thighs. Her lips against his cheek.

"Tell me about this scar," she said, her finger tracing the perfect zig zag through his brow.

She felt his lips curve in a grin. "Landon. She got pissed at me for something I don't even remember. Chucked a Nerf gun at my face. The trigger got caught and ripped open my eyebrow."

"I figured it'd be Carter."

"You don't know my sister."

He pressed a kiss to her jaw. Then her lips. His tongue pushed inside and lazily stroked hers. She melted against him, into him. "I thought of this so many times with you," she whispered. "But it was never like this."

"Better, I hope?" he whispered back, voice filled with amusement.

"Much better. But scarier."

"You never have to be scared of me."

"Maybe I'm more scared of myself," she admitted, feeling safe in the dark, with him, for a little while.

"You wreck me, Presley. I'll never hurt you again."

"How do you know?"

"I just do." He kissed her again, his fingers gripping her scalp, his leg sliding hers apart. "You remind me of the Whitman poem from *I Sing The Body Electric*."

"Tell me a line," she urged against his lips. She rolled to her back and he eased on top of her. Hard again, he slipped inside. Her flesh squeezed tight, keeping him close, and she stared into his eyes.

He recited the stanza with each perfect, deep, slow thrust.

"Hair, bosom, hips, bend of legs, negligent falling hands—all diffused . . . mine too diffused,"

Another thrust. A moan from her lips. Gazes locked.

"Ebb stung by the flow, and flow stung by the ebb . . . loveflesh swelling and deliciously aching,"

Harder, deeper. Body tightening, poised for release. Nails digging into his flesh.

"Limitless limpid jets of love hot and enormous . . . quivering jelly of love . . . white-blow and delirious juice."

Teeth sinking into her lower lip. The orgasm flowing through her in gentle, thorough waves, washing away the doubts, the pain, the past. Bodies sweat-soaked and hot.

187

Collapsing back onto the sheets. The ripe scent of lovemaking drifting in the air.

His lips back on hers. Hands in her hair. Closing eyes in the dark.

"I love you," he breathed.

She slept.

CHAPTER 25

"Morning."

Nolan watched a range of expressions flicker over her face when she opened her eyes.

Satisfaction.

Confusion.

Panic.

Ah, shit.

He should've known the morning after with the woman he loved wouldn't be easy. He'd had easy for too long.

Easy was overrated.

"M-morning. What time is it?"

"Seven a.m. I was hoping I could tempt you to stay for breakfast, but I wasn't sure what your schedule was for work. Didn't want you to oversleep."

God, she was gorgeous. She looked like a sated, well-fucked woman. Bed head hair. Razor burn on her cheeks. Swollen lips.

The scent of him imprinted all over her skin and tangled in his sheets. He wanted her in his damn bed forever. Unfortunately, it looked as if the realization of what they'd done together, along with his late-night soul confession, had struck. Seemed like she may be doing some major back pedaling.

He was ready for it.

Keeping the sheet firmly tucked over her breasts, she sat up, absently gnawing on her lower lips. "I gotta go."

"Not before your coffee, sweetheart. Besides getting cranky as hell, you won't be awake enough to do a thing. How about some fresh fruit, and caffeine? Then I'll drive you home."

Her eyes widened. "No! I can . . . I can take a cab."

His gaze narrowed. "I'm driving you home."

Her lips pursed and she squinted, probably trying to see without her glasses. "You're not the boss of me, beer man."

He tamped down on his laugh, liking her morning sass. She was like a growly bear he wanted to tame. "Of course not. I just want you to get safely home without doing the public walk of shame."

A gasp broke from her lips, but he walked out of the room, allowing himself to finally grin. He heard a stream of mumbling behind him. He fetched her a mug of coffee, dousing it with vanilla soy milk and some cinnamon, then brought it in. She'd managed to get her shirt on in the short amount of time, must've decided to dive back under the covers since her under-wear was hanging on the lamp at the opposite side of the room where he'd tossed it last night.

Good. She was his prisoner for a bit.

He handed her the mug and her glasses, which got him a muttered *thank you*, and he sat on the chair by the bed, watching her drink. The silence settled and stretched between them. Nolan waited her out, content to just study her in the morning light. Finally, color seeped back into her cheeks, and her eyes seemed to focus.

"Better?" he asked.

"Yes. I have to get dressed."

He quirked a brow. "Okay."

She glared. "So, you have to leave."

"After touching and tasting every inch of your delectable body in the dark? Hell, no." He leaned back and crossed an ankle over his leg. "You have no panties on. A man would have to be stupid to leave now."

Her glare got more evil. "We need to move on from last night. I've been thinking. Now, that we did it—"

"Made love?"

She jerked. Thank God, he caught the expression of naked vulnerability and need on her face before she tucked it away. Her walls were just about to crumble, but Presley Cabot was a warrior, and she'd fight to the very last breath.

God, he was crazy about her.

"Had our re-do," she corrected. "We should probably agree to slow down. Back it up. Wait to see if we really are matched for a future type of relationship. Confirm we're both in a solid, good place. Be reasonable."

"Do you remember what I told you last night?" She dipped her head and buried her face in her coffee mug. He caught a brief mumble. "What was that?"

She cleared her throat and spoke louder. "We were caught up in the moment. I won't hold what you said against you."

Now that just pissed him off. He regarded her with a hard

stare, tapping his finger against his knee in steady rhythm. "Bullshit."

Her head flew up and her hand jerked the mug. "What?"

"I call bullshit. Bullshit on you, bullshit on your neat little morning after speech, and bullshit on your kindness for allowing me to take it back. Bull. Shit. I meant every fucking word of what I said, and you owe me a response. An honest one."

"You can't do that!" she accused. "You can't love me! I'm letting you off the hook!"

"It's too late, Presley. I love you. I. Fucking. Love. *You*. And if you don't think that's scary as hell to say to a woman who refuses to accept it, try being in my place." He shook his head and let out a short laugh. "Then again, I probably wouldn't have it any way. Because it's you, and I'll take what I can get."

Her lower lip trembled. Even from the distance, he caught the slight sheen in her eyes. "You can't," she said in a raw whisper. "It's too soon."

He smiled at her. "It feels like our story has always been there, just waiting to be opened to the right chapter to finish it. I feel like I've been making my way toward you my whole life. So, no, it doesn't feel rushed or quick at all. It feels right. Soulmates kind of right."

"You don't know the real me."

His heart shattered at the confusion on her face. He got up from the chair and moved to the bed, sitting beside her, cupping her cheeks in his palms. "Sweetheart, I don't think you realize you're the same person who walked into my bar and threw my world into chaos. That sexy, brave, challenging woman is you. The one who fell and tore her dress and bashed my teeth in? That's you. The one who told me her innermost secrets during a bookstore lunch? All you. And the one in pig slippers with nerd glasses and a bad temper? You, again. It's time you accept all of the parts of yourself, Presley Cabot."

He looked into her beautiful, agonized stormy gray eyes and knew he had to give her the space needed to figure out what they had. That they were meant to be together. That he was worthy of her trust. That they were both worthy of a second chance.

He stroked her hair. "I didn't mean to upset you, but you needed to know. Get dressed and I'll drive you home. You can think about this all you want. You can analyze our past and our present and our future. You can take as much time as you need. I'll still be here, waiting."

He pressed a kiss to her trembling lips.

Then he walked out of the room, praying his gamble would pay off, praying this was not *game over*.

"He said the words? I love you? He said those three exact words?" Libby asked.

"Was it in the throes of orgasm?" Aubrey asked.

Presley sighed and stared at her iPhone. Aubrey and Libby's faces were on the screen. They were both away on business again, and she needed to tell them this latest crisis ASAP. Both of them had ditched their meetings to take her call. "After orgasm. But it was close enough so I figured it didn't count. This morning, I tried to let him take it back but he refused. Said his declaration was true and he loved me. Then he kissed me, told me he'd give me all the time I need, and drove me home."

Libby sighed. "That is so damn romantic. Romance novel romantic."

"It kind of is," Aubrey agreed. "God, he even kind of quoted the bullshit line from *How To Lose a Guy In Ten Days*. I think he's for real, Pres. Why didn't you tell him how you felt?"

Presley shut her eyes. "I panicked," she admitted. "Full-fledge morning-after panic attack. I got a flashback to the first time we slept together and he blew me off. Guess I'm still trying to protect myself."

"From love?" Libby asked. "That's silly."

Aubrey spoke up. "Listen, I'd be the first one to say take it slow and see what happens, but I think you already know the truth. You've been in love with him your whole life. You just have to go and claim his ass."

Presley laughed. "Yeah, I know you're right. I have to head into Manhattan today for back to back meetings. He said when I was ready he'd be waiting."

"Swoon city," Libby said.

"Most importantly, though, how was the sex? Did he make it up to you?" Aubrey asked.

She smiled real slow, glowing with the memories. "Five times worth."

Her friends whooped with congratulations. After a few more encouraging words, they clicked off.

Presley dropped her phone and thought about last night.

Sheer perfection.

It had been more than sex for her. More than physical. Being with Nolan was like finding the other half of herself, as if she'd never even realized a piece of her soul was missing until she fell into his arms. He was her soulmate.

He'd looked into her eyes and declared to see the real her.

For the first time in her life, she believed him. Even though she felt awkward and scared inside, she was still brave and sexy and badass. So, what would a true badass billionaire female do?

Exactly what Aubrey advised.

Go claim her man.

CHAPTER 26

NOLAN GLANCED AT HIS PHONE AGAIN. NO TEXT. NO RESPONSE to his calls.

Yeah, maybe he'd really freaked her out. Maybe it really was game over.

It'd been two days since their night together. He'd been tempted to knock on her door, but after calling Carter, he agreed with his brother's advice.

He needed to let her have some time and space. Nolan figured he'd give her the weekend. Send her flowers. Then try again on Monday.

The radio silence was bad, though. Agonizing.

Groaning, he tried to re-focus on his latest brew, a deeper IPA with an amber color and some backgrounds of lavender. It was more difficult and needed a lighter touch. The last batch hadn't been up to par, so he was going for the second round, tweaking some notes. The official opening was in two weeks, so he'd be at full staff, with six custom house beers on draft, and a finalized tasting menu. Everything he'd worked so hard for was finally in reach.

He tried to focus on the thought, throwing himself into work, when he realized there was some type of music drifting from the window. He frowned, moving out of the brewery to the front of the bar to see what was going on.

The music got louder, the searing notes at full volume, blaring in perfect melody.

WTF?

Barry Manilow? Really?

He flung open the door.

And saw her.

She was standing on the sidewalk, holding a giant, battered boom box over her head. Barry belted out *This One's for You* in old-time glory. She stood before him in all her magnificence, stripped down and vulnerable and raw.

No make-up.

Glasses.

Messy hair.

Jeans. T-shirt. Sneakers.

His heart stopped, sputtered, and kicked back into high gear. He stumbled closer, his ears roaring with the notes of the song that sounded better than any Mozart or Italian opera. They stared at one another while Barry reached his crescendo, then drifted away into a beautiful, shattering silence.

The boom box clicked. She lowered it down and set it on the ground beside her. Her voice was loud and strong when she spoke.

"I'm not running away."

He almost choked with emotion and laughter. Leave it to her to quote him the lines from a damn romantic comedy. Still, he knew his response well. "Bullshit."

He savored her beautiful face, reflecting laughter and longing, just inches away from him. "I don't need any more time, Nolan."

The joy began deep in his gut and spread out to his whole body, invading his blood, filling up his soul, calming his mind. "You didn't return my phone calls," he said.

She took a step closer, her blue-gray eyes gleaming with emotion. "I had an author crisis and I wanted to do this in person. Not over text. I'm an old-fashioned sort of girl. I like DVDs, records, and photographs you can touch and feel. I love romance novels and romantic comedies. I like Barry Manilow."

He took a step forward. "I'm glad, because that would've been a deal breaker."

"You were right. I freaked. And though technically, we've only had a handful of dates, I feel like I've known you my whole life. It's always been you, beer man. I love you, too."

One more step. They stood inches apart. The space between their bodies practically crackled and sizzled with energy. He breathed in her scent, studied her face, soaked in her closeness.

"About damn time, Presley Cabot. Now let's finish this romcom. Come kiss me."

She did.

Thank you for reading The Charm of You – I truly hope you enjoyed! I'd love for you to sign up for my newsletter at www.jenniferprobst.com/newsletter for monthly prizes and exclusive excerpts of all my upcoming releases. I never over-burden your inbox, and love responding to all reader mail. You can find me everywhere on social media. As always, reviews are always appreciated.

Now, here's some sneak peeks and excerpts for you to enjoy!

Searching for Mine

Searching for Disaster

The Billionaire Marriage Series

The Marriage Bargain

The Marriage Trap

The Marriage Mistake

The Marriage Merger

The Book of Spells

The Marriage Arrangement

The Steele Brothers Series

Catch Me

Play Me

Dare Me

Beg Me

Reveal Me

Sex on the Beach Series

Beyond Me

Chasing Me

The Hot in the Hamptons Series

Summer Sins

Stand-Alone Novels

Dante's Fire

ABOUT JENNIFER PROBST

Jennifer Probst wrote her first book at twelve years old. She bound it in a folder, read it to her classmates, and hasn't stopped writing since. She holds a masters in English Literature and lives in the beautiful Hudson Valley in upstate New York. Her family keeps her active, stressed, joyous, and sad her house will never be truly clean. Her passions include horse racing, Scrabble, rescue dogs, Italian food, and wine—not necessarily in that order.

She is the New York Times, USA Today, and Wall Street Journal bestselling author of sexy and erotic contemporary romance. She was thrilled her book, The Marriage Bargain, spent 26 weeks on the New York Times. Her work has been translated in over a dozen countries, sold over a million copies, and was dubbed a "romance phenom" by Kirkus Reviews. She is also a proud three-time RITA finalist.

She loves hearing from readers. Visit her website for updates on new releases and her street team at www.jennifer-probst.com.

Sign up for her newsletter at www.jenniferprobst.com/newsletter for a chance to win a gift card each month and receive exclusive material and giveaways.

Want more from the Ladies Who Write?

www.ladieswhowrite.com

Join our group and help us create a world and stories you want to read about! Look for Aubrey and Libby's story coming soon and make sure you sign up for the newsletter for all the fun info: Newsletter – https://ladieswhowrite.com/newsletter/

Is there a secondary character in **The Charm of You** who deserves their own story?

Come share your thoughts and vote on who will be in the next book. Carter? Trinity? Cam? Landon?

Or a mystery character you brainstorm with us?

Join us at our Reader's Group where we talk about all the things!

Facebook – https://www.facebook.com/LadiesWhoWrite

ACKNOWLEDGMENTS

A special shout-out to these two members from the Ladies Who Write Reader's group who helped brainstorm specific parts of The Charm of You!

Gina Jones – for naming the Port Hudson bookstore – Books n' Crannies

Reina Torres – for the fabulous secondary character of Cam Fong.

Well done, ladies!

Looking forward to many more brainstorming sessions with the group!

DISCOVER MORE JENNIFER PROBST!

The Billionaire Builder Series
Available now!
Everywhere and Every Way – Book 1

Discover this HGTV inspired sexy series who give the Property Brothers a run for their money. These red-hot contractor siblings are at the top of their game—except when it comes to love...

Ever the responsible eldest brother, Caleb Pierce started working for his father's luxury contracting business at a young age, dreaming of one day sitting in the boss's chair. But his father's will throws a wrench in his plans by stipulating that Caleb share control of the family business with his two estranged brothers.

Things only get more complicated when demanding high-end home designer Morgan hires Caleb to build her a customized dream house that matches her specifications to a T

—or she'll use her powerful connections to poison the Pierce brothers' reputation. Not one to ignore a challenge, Caleb vows to get the job done—if only he can stop getting distracted by his new client's perfect...amenities.

But there's more to icy Morgan than meets the eye. And Caleb's not the only one who knows how to use a stud-finder. In fact, Morgan is pretty sure she's found hers—and he looks quite enticing in a hard hat. As sparks fly between Morgan and Caleb despite his best intentions not to mix business and pleasure, will she finally warm up and help him lay the foundation for everlasting love?

PROLOGUE

Caleb Pierce craved a cold beer, air-conditioning, his dogs, and maybe a pretty brunette to warm his bed.

Instead, he got lukewarm water, choking heat, his head in an earsplitting vice, and a raging bitch testing his temper.

And it was only eight a.m.

"I told you a thousand times I wanted the bedroom for my mother off the garage." Lucy Weatherspoon jabbed her French-manicured finger at the framing and back at the plans they'd changed twelve times. "I need her to have privacy and her own entrance. If this is the garage, why is the bedroom off the other side?"

He reminded himself again that running your own company had its challenges. One of them was clients who thought building a house was like shopping at the mall. Sure, he was used to difficult clients, but Lucy tested even his patience. She spoke to him as if he was a bit dim-witted just because he wore jeans with holes in them and battered work boots and had dust covering every inch of his body. His gut had told him to turn down the damn job of building her dream house, but his stubborn father overruled him, calling her congressman husband and telling him Pierce Brothers would be fucking *thrilled* to take on the project. His father always did have a soft spot for power. Probably figured the politician would owe him a favor.

Yeah, Cal would rather have a horse head in his bed than deal with Congressman Weatherspoon's wife.

He wiped the sweat off his brow, noting the slight wrinkle of her nose telling him he smelled. For fun, he deliberately took a step closer to her. "Mrs. Weatherspoon, we went over this several times, and I had you sign off. Remember? Your mother's bedroom has to be on the other side of the house because you decided you wanted the billiard room to be accessed from the garage. Of course, I can add it to the second floor with a private entry, but we'd need to deal with a staircase or elevator."

"No. I want it on the ground floor. I don't remember signing off on this. Are you telling me I need to choose between my mother and the pool table room?"

He tried hard not to gnash his teeth. He'd already lost too much of the enamel, and they'd just broken ground on this job. "No. I'm saying if we put the bedroom on the other side of the house, it won't break the architectural lines, and you can have everything you want. Just. Like. We. Discussed."

She tapped her nude high-heeled foot, studying him as if trying to decipher whether he was a sarcastic asshole or just didn't understand how to talk to the natives. He gave his best dumb look, and finally she sighed. "Fine. I'll bend on this."

Oh, goody.

"But I changed my mind on the multilevel deck. I found this picture on Houzz and want you to recreate it." She shoved a glossy printout of some Arizona-inspired massive patio that was surrounded by a desert. And yep, just as he figured, it was from a spa hotel, which looked nothing like the lake-view property he was currently building on. Knowing it would look ridiculous on the elegant colonial that rivaled a Southern plantation, he forced himself to nod and pretend to study the picture.

"Yes, we can definitely discuss this. Since the deck won't affect my current framing, let's revisit when we begin designing the outside."

That placated her enough to get her to smile stiffly. "Very well. Oh, I'd better go. I'm late for the charity breakfast. I'll check in with you later, Caleb."

"Great." He nodded as she picked her way carefully over the building site and watched her pull away in her shiny black Mercedes. Cal shook his head and gulped down a long drink of water, then wiped his mouth with the back of his hand. Next time, he'd get his architect Brady to deal with her. He was good at charming an endless array of women when they drew up plans, but was never around to handle the temper tantrums on the actual job.

Then again, Brady had always been smarter than him.

Cal did a walk-through to check on his team. The pounding sounds of classic Aerosmith blared from an ancient radio that had nothing on those fancy iPods. It had been on hundreds of jobs with him, covered in grime, soaked with water, battered by falls, and never stopped working. Sure, when he ran, he liked those wireless contraptions, but Cal always felt as if he was born a few decades too late. To him, simple was better. Simple worked just fine, but the more houses he built, the more he was surrounded by requests for fancier equipment, for endless rooms that would never be used, and for him to clear land better left alone.

He nodded to Jason, who was currently finishing up the framing, and ran his hand over the wood, checking for stability and texture. His hands were an extension of all his senses, able to figure out weak spots hidden in rotted wood or irregular length. Of course, he wasn't as gifted as his youngest brother, Dalton, who'd been dubbed the Wood Whisperer. His middle brother, Tristan, only laughed and suggested wood be changed to *woody* to be more accurate. He'd always been the wiseass out of all of them.

Cal wiped the thought of his brothers out of his head, readjusted his hard hat, and continued his quick walk-through. In the past year, Pierce Brothers Construction had grown, but Cal refused to sacrifice quality over his father's constant need to be the biggest firm in the Northeast.

On cue, his phone shrieked, and he punched the button. "Yeah?"

"Cal? Something happened."

The usually calm voice of his assistant, Sydney, broke over the line. In that moment, he knew deep in his gut that everything would change: like the flash of knowledge before a car crash, or the sharp cut of pain before a loss penetrated the brain. Cal tightened his grip on the phone and waited. The heat of the morning pressed over him. The bright blue sky, streaked with clouds, blurred his vision. The sounds of Aerosmith, drills, and hammers filled his ears.

"Your father had a heart attack. He's at Haddington Memorial."

"Is he okay?"

Sydney paused. The silence told him everything he needed to know and dreaded to hear. "You need to get there quick."

"On my way."

Calling out quickly to his team, he ripped off his hat, jumped into his truck, and drove.

A mass of machines beeped, and Cal tried not to focus on the tubes running into his father's body in an attempt to keep him alive. They'd tried to keep him out by siccing security on him and making a scene, but he refused to leave until they allowed him to stand beside his bed while they prepped him for surgery.

Christian Pierce was a hard, fierce man with a force that pushed through both opposition and people like a tank. At seventy years old, he'd only grown more grizzled, in both body and spirit, leaving fear and respect in his wake but little tenderness. Cal stared into his pale face while the machines moved up and down to keep breath in his lungs and reached out tentatively to take his father's hand.

"Get off me, for God's sake. I'm not dying. Not yet."

Cal jerked away. His father's eyes flew open. The familiar coffee-brown eyes held a hint of disdain at his son's weakness, even though they were red rimmed and weary. Cal shoved down the brief flare of pain and arranged his face to a neutral expression. "Good, because I want you to take over the Weatherspoons. They're a pain in my ass."

His father grunted. "I need some future political favors. Handle it." He practically spit at the nurse hovering and checking his vitals. "Stop poking me. When do I get out of here?"

The pretty blonde hesitated. Uh-oh. His father was the worst patient in the world, and he bit faster than a rattlesnake when cornered. Already, he looked set to viciously tear her to verbal pieces while she seemed to be gathering the right words to say.

Cal saved her by answering. "You're not. Doctor said you need surgery to unblock some valves. They're sending you now."

His father grunted. "Idiot doctor has been wanting me to go under the knife for years. He just wants to make money and shut me up. He's still bitching I overcharged him on materials for his house."

"You did."

"He can afford it."

Cal didn't argue. He knew the next five minutes were vital, before his father was wheeled into surgery. He'd already been told by the serious-faced Dr. Wang that it wouldn't be an easy surgery. Not with his father's previous heart damage from the last attack and the way he'd treated his body in the past few years. Christian liked his whiskey, his cigars, and his privacy. He thought eating healthy and walking on treadmills were for weaklings. When he was actually doing the construction part of the business, he'd been in better shape, but the last decade his father had faded to the office work and wheeling and dealing behind the scenes.

"I'm calling Tristan and Dalton. They need to know."

In seconds, his father raged at him in pure fury. "You will not. Touch that fucking phone and I'll wipe you out of my will."

Cal gave him a hard stare, refusing to flinch. "Go ahead. Been looking to work at Starbucks anyway."

"Don't mock me. I don't want to deal with their guilt or bullshit. I'll be fine, and we both know it."

"Dad, they have a right to know."

"They walked out on me. They have a right to know nothing." A thin stream of drool trickled from his mouth. Cal studied the slow trek, embarrassed his father couldn't control it. Losing bodily functions would be worse than death for his father. He needed to come out of this surgery in one whole piece, or he didn't know what would happen.

Ah, shit, he needed to call his brothers. His father made a mule look yogic. They might have had a falling-out, and not spoken for too long, but they were still family. The hell with it. He'd contact them as soon as his father went into surgery—it was the right thing to do.

Christian half rose from the pillow. "Don't even think about going behind my back, boy. I have ways of making your life hell beyond the grave, and if I wake up and they're here, I'll make sure you regret it."

Again, that brief flare of pain he had no right to feel. How long had he wished his father would show him a sliver of softness? Any type of warmer emotion? Instead, he'd traded those feelings for becoming a drill sergeant with his boys, the total opposite of the way Mom had been. Not that he wanted to think of her anymore. It did no good except scrape against raw wounds. Caleb wasn't a martyr, so he stuffed that shit back down for another lifetime.

"Whatever, old man. Save the fight for the surgery."

They were interrupted when the Dr. Wang came in with an easy smile. "Okay, gentlemen, this is it. We gotta wheel him into surgery. Say your good-byes."

Caleb froze and stared into his father's familiar face. Took in the sharp, roughened features, leathery skin, bushy silver brows. Those brown eyes still held a fierce spark of life. In that moment, Caleb decided to take a chance. If something happened in surgery, he didn't want to regret it for the rest of his life.

He leaned down to kiss his father on the cheek.

Christian slapped him back with a growl. "Cut it out. Grow some balls. I'll see you later."

The tiny touch of emotion flickered out and left a cold, empty vastness inside his belly. So stupid. He felt so stupid. "Sure. Good luck, Dad."

"Don't need no damn luck. Make sure you do what I say. I don't want to see your brothers."

They were the last words Caleb heard as his father was wheeled into a surgery that took over five hours to perform.

The next morning Christian Pierce was dead.

And then the nightmare really began.

BUY EVERYWHERE AND EVERY WAY HERE:
https://books2read.com/u/mvKyRl

The Start of Something Good: Available now!
Discover the brand new STAY series!
An enriching story of family ties, broken hearts, and second chances from *New York Times* bestselling author Jennifer Probst.

When Ethan Bishop returns to the Hudson Valley, his body and spirit are a little worse for wear. As a former Special Forces paratrooper, he saw his fair share of conflict, and he came home with wounds, inside and out. At his sisters' B & B and farm, he can keep all his pain at a safe distance. But quiet time isn't easy when a fiery woman explodes into his life...

It's business—not pleasure—that brings Manhattan PR agent Mia Thrush reluctantly to the farm. Tightly wound and quick tempered, Mia clashes immediately with the brooding Ethan. Everything about him is irritating—from his lean muscles and piercing blue eyes to his scent of sweat and musk.

But as the summer unfolds and temperatures rise, Ethan and Mia discover how much they have in common: their guarded histories, an uncontrollable desire, and a passion for the future that could heal two broken hearts. But will their pasts threaten their fragile chance at a brand-new future?

CHAPTER ONE

His feet knew the road ahead like a long lost memory, but this time, Ethan Bishop had to pause halfway to rest. The nagging, ache throbbed behind his knee like a deeply ingrained splinter, slowly trying to drive him mad, but he packaged the pain into a box and shoved it down deep, along with the hot flare of shame.

He was the lucky one.

The mantra had been repeated regularly for the last thirty-two days, yet still felt like words recited in a play, to someone he was pretending to be. No matter. Eventually, he may believe them.

He shifted his weight and stared at the sprawling blue and white farmhouse, hidden behind the storybook white fence, and framed by the majestic Shawangunk mountains. His heart stopped, stuttered, then began beating again. He'd forgotten how long he'd been away from home. A rush of memories washed over him like a tide of warm water, reminding him of that laughing, free-spirited young kid tearing his way around the farm with big dreams that his small upstate town could never hold. After years of hard work and chasing those elusive ambitions, he thought he'd finally succeeded.

He'd been so wrong.

Gritting his teeth, he resumed walking, taking in the extensive updates with approval. His sisters had invested a large chunk of money to not only renovate the actual house, but freshen up the visual curb appeal of the bed & breakfast. The new *Robin's Nest B&B* sign welcomed visitors from the gate in blinding white and robin blue, matching the shutters and bold blue door. As he approached the wraparound porch, he noticed the creative touches Ophelia must have spearheaded—from the clay pots of colored mums, tea cart filled with pitchers of sweet tea and sugar cookies, to the wind chimes tinkling in the soft summer breeze. The rockers and footstools were charmingly mismatched in various wicker, and large coffee table books with glossy pictures were casually thrown about.

Yes, they'd finally claimed their heritage just as he'd run from it. Mom would have been proud.

The familiar bark rose to his ears, and he turned in astonishment, dropping his bag. The black lab tore across the lawn, ears pinned back, mouth turned up in a joyous doggy grin, and barreled into his arms.

"Wheezy!" The dog stuck a wet nose in between his crotch and a laugh exploded in the air. It took him a while to realize it had come from him, the sound rusty from disuse. Ethan ran his fingers over now whitish fur wriggling in delight, his belly now rounded with the extra weight of middle age. "I missed you, boy. God, how old are you now, buddy? Fourteen? Fifteen?"

"Sixteen. And in better shape than all of us. Welcome home, Ethan."

He craned his neck around. Ophelia stood on the porch, her lips curved in a soft smile. She was dressed in an ankle length floral skirt, sandals, and a white gauzy tank top, showing off her willowy form. Her strawberry blonde hair was pulled back from her face in a ponytail. She'd always reminded him of a fairy, with her pointed chin, too-large eyes, and petite build. Of course, his sister had an inner strength and thirst for life like no other he'd ever known, hidden behind a Tinkerbell surface. Once, he'd imagined she'd be bigger than Adele, with her giant voice that mesmerized anyone in her vicinity, but it seemed she'd decided to settle for running the family bed and breakfast.

"Tink. You look good."

She groaned, taking the few steps down to close the distance. "Don't call me that! It was torturous enough when we were kids—I refuse to accept it as an adult."

He grabbed her, lifting high and enjoying her laugh as he spun her around and Wheezy barked. "I can still make you fly," he said, pressing a kiss to the top of her head. "And older brothers have a responsibility to annoy their younger siblings."

"Fine. Have I told you I put your room next to Mr. & Mrs. Alders? They're in their seventies and celebrating their anniversary." Her blue eyes danced. "Very loudly. Every night."

He shuddered. "You fight dirty, Tink. No way am I staying in a house full of strangers. I told you I'm setting up in the bungalow."

"I was hoping I'd change your mind," she said lightly. "The bungalow doesn't have a full working kitchen. The place is run down and needs a bunch of updates. No one's been in there for years."

"Doesn't bother me as long as there's a bed or a couch."

"It's isolated. Plus, it's a long walk to the main house."

He narrowed his gaze, getting closer to the truth. She shifted her weight and fussed with her skirt. "You worried about something else?"

At least, she didn't lie to him. "I'm worried about leaving you alone."

The words fell between them and lay there like broken glass. His gut clenched with familiar shame but he ignored it, making sure to keep his voice firm. "I came back so I could be alone for a bit. Need to get my shit together. Can't think of a better job than fixing up the bungalow and spending some time helping you out."

She seemed to mull over his words to figure out if he was lying. Then, she nodded. "Okay. Does it hurt?"

"Not much. Just need to continue some PT."

"Therapy?"

The corner of his lip lifted. Ever since the incident, not many people asked straight out questions that may embarrass them or him. His muscles relaxed a bit, glad his sister wouldn't treat him any differently. "Did my mandated time. If I feel like I need more, I'll find someone."

"Good enough for me. But be careful about telling Harper you have free time. She'll have you working with the horses nonstop so she can rescue more."

"Still saving the world one animal at a time?"

"She's the Angelina Jolie for rescues and pissing off more people than I can count."

"Where is she?"

"At the auction. She'll be home for dinner. In the meantime, why don't you get settled in and I can show you around. We've done a lot of improvements." She eyed the duffle bag at his feet. "Is that all you have?"

"I learned to travel light. Do we have to eat with your guests?"

She grinned. "Not tonight. But we have quite a crew for the week. I think you're going to like them."

"I hate talking to people, Tink."

"Yet you've always charmed everyone in your path," she flung back. "And part of your job here is to make the guests happy. Better start getting used to it."

He groaned but she only shot him a wink and disappeared back into the house.

Ethan stood in the hot sun, thinking about the life he'd run far away from for something bigger and better. He'd finally come full circle—back in the place he started in order to heal all the broken pieces life had thrown at him. So fucking ironic.

As if Wheezy knew exactly what he was thinking, the dog regarded him with serious, soulful eyes.

Then he lifted his leg and peed on Ethan's bag.

Welcome home.

Buy The Start of Something Good HERE:
https://books2read.com/u/bP5NrR

10624344R00138